At the end of scie   [barcode]   on his desk.

"Okay, everyone. I'd like to make a special announcement. For the next month or so, you're going to have a student teacher, Mr. Monroe. I hope you will all be on your best behavior."

"Oh, great," I whispered to Heather.

"Shhhh!" Heather said. She pointed at the door.

I swiveled around in my seat. Standing in the doorway was the most gorgeous guy I had ever seen in my life! The shape of his face was perfect—not too round and not too square. His dark eyebrows showed off his thick eyelashes and beautiful dark eyes.

"Class," Mr. Norris said, "I'd like to introduce Mr. Monroe."

Mr. Monroe walked to the front of the room. He stopped less than a foot away from me! Our eyes locked. *Please don't look away*, I thought. *I could stare into your eyes forever.*

**Get the inside scoop from
DIARY S.O.S.**

My Sister Stole My Boyfriend

by Megan Howard

BULLSEYE BOOKS

Random House 🏠 New York

For Elise

ACKNOWLEDGMENTS

Special thanks to Margot Jaffe, DDS, and her staff

Produced by Daniel Weiss Associates, Inc.,
33 West 17th Street, New York, NY 10011.

Library of Congress Catalog Card Number: 93-85683
ISBN: 0-679-85703-6

RL: 4.8

First Bullseye Books edition: June 1994

Manufactured in the United States of America   10 9 8 7 6 5 4 3 2 1

New York, Toronto, London, Sydney, Auckland

Chapter 1

Dear Diary,

So far, 7th grade is much better than elementary school, but not as great as it could be. I thought for sure that I'd have a boyfriend by now—Jake Meadows, to be specific. He's the most gorgeous guy at Whitman Junior High—the nicest, too. Unfortunately, he's going out with Shannon Sommer, the most stuck-up girl in the school. Bleh!

I wish Yvonne hadn't gone away to college and left me with Anne the Alien Sister. Yvonne gives great guy advice—and she knows how to make me feel better. I still talk

to her on the phone a lot,
but it's just not the same.

*   -R*

"We were beginning to think you weren't going to come," I told Amy Leonard as she sat down across the table from Heather Cohen and me. As usual, Amy was late. Heather and I had already been at the Pop Stop, the most popular hangout in Englewood, for half an hour.

"Sorry," Amy shouted over the music blaring from the video jukebox monitors. "Dad and I were shooting hoops at the Community Center gym. We kind of lost track of the time."

Heather adjusted her glasses on her nose. "Did you win?"

"Yup. Two games to one. And he didn't let me win either." Amy tightened the red elastic around her blond ponytail. "Sweat was just *dripping* down his face."

I scrunched up my nose. "Oooh, gross." I hate everything about sports—*especially* sweating.

Amy giggled. "So what have you guys been talking about?"

"I've been testing Rosie's problem-solving skills," Heather said, showing Amy the book of brainteasers we were using.

"Yeah, it's really fun," I told her.

Heather leaned toward Amy. "Of course it's fun for *her*. She's gotten every single question right," she said. "The master problem solver."

"Tell me about it," Amy said. "Rosie's always coming up with great solutions—to get out of all the messes she gets herself into." She and Heather started laughing, so I stuck out my tongue at them. But I had to laugh too.

Amy and I have been best friends since the summer before fourth grade. That's when my family moved to Virginia from Jamaica. Amy lived right next-door and was in my fourth-grade class. She stuck by me when some of the kids at school made fun of my Jamaican accent.

Getting to be best friends with Heather was another story. Heather and her mom had moved to Englewood from a farm outside of town right before school started this year. Of course, Amy made her feel welcome right away. I got pretty jealous of their friendship, so I was mean to both of them. Luckily, Amy, Heather, and I made up, and now the three of us are best friends.

"Next question, please," I announced, waving a french fry in the air like a wand.

"Here's one that I bet will stump you." Heather pushed her brown hair behind her ear and read from the page. "A little boy is rushed into the emergency room at the hospital. He needs surgery immediately. The surgeon who is supposed to operate looks at the boy and says, 'I can't operate on this child. He's my son.' The surgeon is not the boy's father, but the boy is the surgeon's son. Who is the surgeon?"

Amy narrowed her eyes as she thought. "I know!" she said. "It's his stepson."

Heather shook her head. "No, the boy *is* the surgeon's son."

"That's easy," I said. "The surgeon is the boy's *mother*."

"Right!" Heather held a spoon up to her mouth like a microphone. "Now, Amy, tell Miss Banton what she's won for having such outstanding problem-solving skills."

"Well, Miss Banton, a year's supply of napkins"—Amy motioned to the chrome napkin dispenser—"and this handy container are yours."

I put my hands on my cheeks and opened my eyes wide in mock surprise. "Oh, my gosh! Oh, my gosh! This is the proudest moment of my *life*." Amy and Heather cracked up.

"Actually," I said when we stopped giggling, "maybe you guys can help *me* solve a problem. See, my grandparents in Jamaica gave me and my sisters each a hundred dollars—"

"You call that a problem?" Heather broke in.

"The problem is, I have to give half the money to a good cause, and I don't know which one."

Amy shrugged. "If it's gift money, why do you have to give away any of it?"

"Well, it was partly my idea. After Anne, Yvonne, and I helped Mom out at the soup kitchen at our church, I realized how important it is to contribute to good causes. So I kind of suggested it. I'm spending fifty dollars on a new outfit. I'd like to use the rest to help the environment, but I don't know which organization to donate it to."

I've been really into the environment since I sort of accidentally joined the environment club at the beginning of the school year. I'd never thought that pollution and garbage could be so interesting. I learned so many different ways to reuse and recycle things, and before I knew it, I was elected club president.

"What about giving your money to save the rain forest?" Heather suggested.

"That's an idea," I said. "We talked about rain forests in a couple of environment club meetings. They're being destroyed so that huge companies can have more land for farming."

"Right," Heather agreed. "When the forests are gone, the whole balance of nature gets out of whack."

"Uh huh," I said, strumming my fingers on the table. "Saving the rain forest would be a great way to spend the fifty bucks. But I don't know where to start."

"I have an idea," Heather said. "In social studies, we read about a group of kids in New York who bought an acre of rain forest."

"There's a rain forest in New York?" Amy asked.

I shook my head. "No, silly, the rain forest is mainly in places near the equator— like South America."

"These kids bought an acre in El Salvador," Heather continued. "Maybe you could buy an acre somewhere."

"That's a good idea," I said. "If someone owns it, no one else can touch it."

"Hey, that's really cool, Rosie," Amy said. "And if you did that, you'd actually own some land, too."

"Yeah. So, how do I do it?" I asked Heather.

"I'll talk to my social studies teacher on Monday," she said.

"Thanks for the suggestion," I said, sipping the last bit of my Lemon Twist. A girl with wavy black hair walked by, carrying a drink. "Hey, there's Lucy." Lucy Cruz lives on the same block as Amy and me.

"That's weird," Amy said. "She usually comes over to say hi."

"Hey, Lucy!" I called.

Lucy turned around and walked to our table.

"Didn't you see us sitting here?" Amy asked.

Lucy put her hand over her mouth and mumbled something.

"What?" I asked.

Lucy dropped her hand and looked at the floor. "I got braces yesterday. They really hurt."

As she spoke, we could see bright red rubber bands wrapped around the braces on her teeth.

"Those rubber bands look really cool," Amy told her.

"One of my friends at my old school got braces last year. Your mouth will probably stop hurting in a couple days," Heather told her.

"I know, but my orthodontist said I can't eat corn on the cob or chew gum for a whole year and a half—longer if I don't wear my headgear."

"What's headgear?" Amy asked. "You mean like a football helmet?"

7

"Might as well be." Lucy reached into her purse and pulled out a weird-looking contraption. It was a couple of narrow strips of shiny metal, curved into semicircles, with a multicolored strap hanging from one side. She slid one metal semicircle into her mouth, with the other circling her cheeks, and hooked the strap around her neck.

She took off the headgear and put it back in her purse. "I have to wear it after school and at night, but at least I can take it off when I eat." She sighed. "I'd better go drink my float before all the ice cream melts."

"Poor Lucy," I whispered as she walked to the table where her best friend, Kristen Pagano, was sitting. "I'd die if I had to wear braces."

"It's not so bad," Heather said. "The colored rubber bands are pretty cool. Besides, her teeth will look great when the braces come off."

"What about that awful headgear?" I reminded her. "And her mouth is killing her." I squirmed in my seat at the thought of all that pain.

Amy nudged me. "Don't look now, Rosie, but guess who just showed up!" she whispered excitedly.

I glanced toward the entrance, where Jake

Meadows was standing. He looked as gorgeous as always. He has light brown hair, a dimple in each cheek, and a really muscular body. He was wearing his purple letter jacket. Jake makes purple, my favorite color, look extra great.

I smiled and waved.

"He's coming this way," Heather said.

"Hey, you guys," Jake greeted us. "What's up?"

"We're helping Rosie buy a rain forest," Amy said quickly. That was typical Amy—she didn't want to tell him about the braces so Lucy wouldn't be embarrassed.

Jake's eyes grew wide. "You're buying a rain forest?"

"Well, part of one," I explained. "I'm going to buy a piece so that big companies can't ruin it."

"Wow! That's really cool."

"I just think it's important to save the earth before it's too late."

"Yeah, I—"

"Jake! Over here!" My heart dropped as Shannon and her group of loud, pretty—and obnoxious—friends came into the Pop Stop. Jake turned and smiled at her, as though he'd completely forgotten about me and the environment.

"See you guys at school tomorrow," Jake said as he walked toward Shannon's table.

Amy wiggled her head like Shannon. "Jake! Over here!" she mimicked in a high, screechy voice.

"Jake's way too nice for Shannon. Why does he always obey her like she's the queen of England?" Heather asked.

"I don't know," I said. "But I'm getting pretty tired of trying to compete with Her Majesty."

Dear Diary,

I can't believe I'm saying this, but maybe I should just give up on Jake. It's so hard, since I know we're a perfect match-but I'm beginning to think that he's never going to realize it.

My heart feels like someone took it right out of my chest. I guess I'll just have to admit that Shannon really has me beat. I'll never get over Jake. There will never be anyone like him.

-R

Chapter 2

"What's this slide?" I asked Amy and Heather as I looked through the microscope lens during science class. It's the only class that the three of us have together.

Heather glanced at the worksheet Mr. Norris had handed out. "Epidermis."

"Epi-*what*?" Amy asked.

"It's another word for skin," Heather told her.

"Yuck! That's disgusting," Amy said. She clutched her throat and pretended to gag.

I giggled and shook my head. "You have skin all over your body."

"Where it's supposed to be." She took a few steps back from the table and folded her arms.

Heather took her turn studying the slide and sketching what she saw. "Your turn, Amy," she said when she had finished.

"I'll just copy your pictures. It'll be faster that way anyway." She picked up a pencil, looked at our papers, and started to draw.

"Amy," I said, rolling my eyes. "How do you expect to learn anything?" I'd let Amy copy work from me in elementary school, but that was different. Seventh-grade science was real science. We got to use scientific equipment like Bunsen burners, beakers, and microscopes. And Mr. Norris was a real scientist. I wasn't going to help Amy cheat on something so serious.

"Okay, okay," Amy said, defeated, as she leaned to look into the microscope.

"Oh, I almost forgot," Heather told me. "I talked to my social studies teacher about those kids who bought the rain forest. She gave me the name of an organization you can mail a donation to."

"Great!" I said. "I can't believe I'll be the owner of an entire acre of rain forest."

Heather shook her head. "There's a *slight* problem. An acre of rain forest costs at least a hundred dollars."

"A hundred dollars?" Amy and I said together.

"But you don't have to buy an acre yourself," Heather said. "You can just donate your fifty dollars, and they'll combine it with money that other people donate."

"I don't like that idea so much," I decided. "It wouldn't be the same if my acre belonged to a bunch of strangers, too. Then it wouldn't feel like *I* was really saving it. I've got to come up with fifty more dollars."

"Well, you could always use *all* the money from your grandparents," Heather suggested.

I shook my head. "I don't want to sound selfish or anything, but fifty dollars is a lot for me to give up to begin with."

"Why don't you collect aluminum cans and glass bottles and take them down to the recycling center?" Amy suggested. "A lot of people will let you take their recycling for them and keep the money. Simon's Cub Scout den made more than a hundred dollars that way." Simon is Amy's ten-year-old brother.

"Amy and I could help you," Heather added.

"Rosie, Heather, and Amy's Acre," I announced. "I like the way that sounds."

"I thought you didn't want to share your acre with other people," Amy pointed out.

"That was with complete strangers. It would be really cool if *we* owned an acre together."

"Yeah, it would be awesome," Amy agreed.

"I think we're forgetting something, you guys," Heather said. "Simon's den has at least fifteen kids in it. There are just three of us."

Amy put her chin in her hands. "Heather's right. I guess it's not such a good plan."

"There has to be some way to make it work," I told them. I tapped my foot on the floor as I thought. "I know," I said finally. "At the environment club meeting this afternoon, we're voting on a community project. I bet if the whole club pitched in we could find a lot of cans and bottles lying in the road and the park. We could clean up Englewood *and* earn enough money to buy an acre of rain forest."

"Probably more than enough," Heather added eagerly.

"I can't wait to tell all the other members."

Mr. Norris rapped his desk. "Okay, everyone," he said loudly. "We have only ten minutes left, and I would like to make a special announcement." Mr. Norris is my favorite teacher. You can tell he's really into teaching science, because he gets so excited about our projects, even though he must have done them a million times already.

"Maybe we're going on a field trip," I whispered to Amy and Heather.

"That'd be great," Amy said. "We'd get to miss some school."

Mr. Norris cleared his throat, and the class grew quiet.

"For the next month, this class will have a student teacher. I will help out, of course, whenever I am needed. Right now Mr. Monroe is waiting in the teacher's lounge. Please sit quietly until I get back."

As soon as Mr. Norris left the room, I leaned toward Amy and Heather. "Great," I complained. "A student teacher probably won't even know what he's talking about."

"Maybe he'll be easier than Mr. Norris," Amy said hopefully.

"I'll tell you what he'll be," I said. "Four feet tall, with high-water pants and stringy hair. That's what all the guys who are into science look like."

"*I* like science," Glen Benedict said. He sits next to Heather, and I've loathed him ever since the first day of school, when I got stuck doing the first lab with him. He goofed around the whole time, and on the very last step he set the experiment on fire.

I rolled my eyes at Glen. "See what I mean?" I said. Although Glen was at least five feet tall, his pants were always an inch too short, and he greased back his black hair with some unidentifiable substance.

"Anyway, it's just not fair," I continued. "Why'd they have to do this to my favorite teacher?"

"Shhh!" Heather said, pointing to the door.

I turned around in my seat. Mr. Norris had come back in, and right behind him was the most gorgeous guy I had ever seen in my life! This was our student teacher? The shape of his face was perfect—not too round and not too square. His dark eyebrows showed off his thick eyelashes and dark eyes. And I could tell that underneath his khaki pants, silky cream-colored shirt, and black jacket, he had fabulous muscles.

"Settle down!" Mr. Norris said to the class. "I'd like to introduce Mr. Monroe."

Mr. Monroe walked to the front of the teacher's desk. He was less than a foot away from me! Our eyes locked. *Please don't look away*, I thought. *I could stare into your eyes forever.*

"I guess I should tell you a little bit about myself," Mr. Monroe said. His voice was wonderfully soft—as though he were speaking only to me. "I'm a senior at Central Virginia Polytechnic Institute. When I graduate in June, I plan to teach junior-high science. This will be my first time teaching, so you'll be teaching me as much as I'll be teaching you." As he spoke, I got lost in his perfect lips—not too pink and not too red.

"Rosie? Yo, Rosie!" Amy snapped me out of my dream.

"What?" I asked, pulling my eyes off our student teacher, who had turned to talk to Mr. Norris.

"Aren't you going to get up? The bell rang."

"Huh?" I looked around. Kids were rushing out of the classroom. "Oh, yeah," I said, getting up.

"It's too bad Mr. Norris won't be teaching us," Heather said as we walked down the hall. "But Mr. Monroe seems all right."

"All right?" I asked. "Mr. Monroe is definitely more than all right."

"What happened to your being upset about having a student teacher?" Amy asked.

"Well...I just think we should give Mr. Monroe a chance. Like he said, we'll be teaching him as much as he'll be teaching us."

"Since when are you into giving teachers a chance?" Amy raised her eyebrows.

I checked out the hall to make sure there were no big-mouthed spies around. "Mr. Monroe is absolutely the best-looking guy I've seen in my life," I whispered.

"I thought *Jake* was the best-looking guy in the world," Amy said.

Heather led us up the steps to the second floor. "According to you and every other girl in the school."

"Please! Compared to Mr. Monroe, Jake's just a kid," I said. "Mr. Monroe's a...a thinking girl's guy."

"A *thinking girl's guy*?" Amy repeated as Heather and I opened our lockers, which are right next to each other.

"I read about it in *Contemporary Teen* last month," I said. *Contemporary Teen* is my favorite magazine. It has the best fashions and great pictures of movie stars and rock bands, and it covers the latest trends. I tried to remember the article I'd read. "Jake is an obvious babe—so lots of girls go for him. But a *thinking* girl has more mature tastes. She looks for intelligence and...undefinable qualities."

"What kind of undefinable qualities?" Heather asked.

"I can't possibly define them. But Mr. Monroe's got them," I sighed dreamily, clutching my social studies book.

"Um, Rosie, aren't you getting a little carried away?" Amy asked. "Mr. Monroe's at least ten years older than you."

"Thinking girls are often too mature for guys their own age," I explained. "Besides, look at my parents. My dad is fifteen years older than my mother. He says she keeps him young."

"Still, you don't know anything about Mr. Monroe," Amy said. "He could be married."

"He doesn't have a ring."

"What about a girlfriend?" Heather added.

"Come on, you guys. He definitely noticed me. Didn't you see him staring at me?"

"Actually, not really," Amy answered.

"Well, he wouldn't be totally obvious about it. After all, I'm his student—for a few weeks, anyway. But once I show him how mature I am, he won't be able to resist me—even though I'm younger."

"How do you plan to do that?" Amy asked suspiciously.

"Well, fabulous clothes for starters." I shut my locker. "I'm going to the mall this afternoon. I want to get my new outfit right away."

Chapter 3

Heather dangled a peach-colored shirt covered with tiny lilac flowers in front of my face. "How about this one?"

"It's nice," I told her, "but it's not mature enough. I'm looking for the kind of clothes Yvonne would wear." I could picture my sister's wardrobe totally impressing Mr. Monroe. Unfortunately, she was nearly three hours away, and I wouldn't be able to borrow anything.

"I've never met Yvonne," Heather reminded me.

"Oh, yeah, I forgot. But that doesn't matter anyway," I told her. "I think I know the problem. Yvonne doesn't shop in juniors anymore. Maybe we should try another department—like women's."

"We just passed through there," Amy groaned. "You can't afford that stuff." She slumped into a chair next to the dressing rooms. "Besides, I'm getting tired. Can't we at least eat something?"

"Okay, let's get some french fries," I suggested.

"Hooray!" Amy shouted, jumping out of her chair. "We're out of here!"

"I wonder what Mr. Monroe's first name is," I said dreamily as we walked past some pants with designer tags hanging from the waistbands. "Calvin?...Perry?"

"How about Ralph?" Heather giggled.

"There is no way that such a gorgeous man is named Ralph," I told her.

"It could be worse," Amy said. "It could be Melvin."

"No...Homer," I added, laughing.

"How about Albert?" Heather asked.

"Well, I don't care if he has the grossest name in the world," I said, stepping onto the down escalator. "I'll still think he's wonderful."

Heather raised an eyebrow. "Okay, but if I were you I wouldn't want to be Mrs. Melvin Monroe."

We stepped off the escalator next to a big display of jungle-print scarves. That's when I remembered my big news. "By the way, guys, the environment club loved my suggestion about recycling—or should I say *your* suggestion. And they want to make you two honorary members."

"Cool," Amy said.

"So can you guys come to our recycling drive on Saturday morning?"

"Sure," Heather agreed. "That sounds like fun."

Amy linked her arms through Heather's and mine, and the three of us skipped by the accessory counters.

Suddenly, among the makeup displays, a big sign caught my eye. I slowed down to read it. AT CHIC COSMETICS, WE WANT TO HELP YOU DISCOVER YOUR INNER BEAUTY. GET A FREE MAKEOVER TODAY. A woman in a pale yellow smock stood next to the sign.

"Why are we stopping?" Amy asked, bouncing on the balls of her feet. "I can almost smell the french fries."

"This won't take very long," I assured her. I pointed to the sign. "I just figured out how to look really mature."

"A makeover?" Amy asked. "No way."

"Your parents said that you couldn't wear

makeup until you're in high school," Heather reminded me.

"But this would be the perfect way to show Mr. Monroe that I'm not a little kid—even if my parents think I am." I looked at the woman in the yellow smock. "I'd like a free makeover."

"Is this for a party?" the woman asked, smiling brightly. Her lips were a deep red, and her eyebrows were two thin lines drawn on with some kind of makeup pencil.

"Just for school."

"Very well. Sit right here." She tapped a silver-and-black stool by the counter.

"At least we finally get to rest," Amy whispered to Heather as they climbed onto the stools next to mine.

"My name is Lenora," the woman told me. "I'll be your beauty facilitator."

"I'm Rosie," I told her.

"What's a beauty facilitator?" Amy asked.

The woman smiled at her.

"Through makeup therapy, I'll help Rosie discover her natural beauty."

"Wouldn't it be more natural if she didn't wear makeup?"

Lenora didn't answer. She reached into a

cabinet and pulled out a huge tray with every kind of makeup you could imagine. Then she dabbed a thick brown liquid onto a triangular sponge. "First, we'll even out your skin tone."

Amy leaned over to get a better look. "It looks pretty even to me already. Rosie hardly ever gets zits."

"Next we'll bring out those gorgeous cheek-bones," Lenora went on, as she stroked a makeup brush across the powder blush.

I sat perfectly still while my beauty facilitator continued to paint and powder my face.

"Now pucker," Lenora said, then pretended to kiss the air.

I puckered while she rubbed rosy pink lipstick across my lips.

"Finished," Lenora said, handing me a mirror.

My eyes nearly popped out of my head. "I look at least nineteen!"

"You do look as though you could be in college," Lenora whispered.

"How much does all this stuff cost?"

Lenora pulled a calculator out of her pocket and punched the numbers. "Ninety-two dollars and sixty-four cents."

"I think it would be a lot cheaper at the drugstore," Heather said quietly.

Lenora shook her head. "Chic products are unique. Cheap drugstore products could destroy Rosie's beautiful complexion."

"Thanks for your help, but we'd better go," Amy said, standing up. She grabbed my arm, pulled me off the stool, and dragged me past the other makeup and jewelry counters. I tried to hold back, but Amy was going too fast. She didn't let me go until we reached the women's hosiery department, where Heather finally caught up with us.

"What did you do that for?" I asked, rubbing my arm where Amy had been holding on.

"Just forget about it, Rosie," she said. "You don't have enough money."

"I have a hundred dollars," I told her, catching my breath.

"You're only supposed to spend *half* of your grandparents' money, remember? The rest is supposed to go to the rain forest."

"You practically pulled my arm out of the socket just to tell me something I already know? Anyway, since you guys came up with that great recycling idea, I probably won't need to contribute all fifty dollars. I'll just collect extra aluminum and glass."

I walked quickly back to Lenora's counter

and plunked my money down. "I'll take everything!" I told her.

When I pushed open the front door, I heard my mom in the kitchen, cooking and singing along to the reggae music on the radio.

I'd scrubbed off all my makeup at Amy's house, so all I had to do was make it past my mom without her asking what was in my bag. She'd have a fit if she knew I'd bought makeup. It was a big rule in our family—no makeup until we were fourteen. So I snuck past the kitchen doorway and tiptoed down the hall.

Safe, I thought, reaching for the doorknob to my bedroom.

"What's that you've got under your arm, Rosie?"

"Aaah!" I screamed at the sound of Nanna's voice.

"You act as if you've just seen a ghost, not your Nanna." Nanna is my mother's mother. She moved in with my family ten years ago, when my grandfather died.

"I didn't see you there." I squeezed the bag tighter in my hands and swallowed the lump in my throat.

"Well?" Nanna said. "What's in the bag?"

"This bag?" I asked, casually glancing down at the pink sack. Nanna nodded. "Um…this is just a bunch of school supplies."

"You used all the supplies your parents bought you at the beginning of the school year?"

"This is for a special English project." I opened my door. "Well, I've got a lot of home-work. I'd better get started." I slipped into my room and shut the door.

"Rosie!" I heard my mother calling from down the hall.

Going into emergency panic mode, I shoved the bag of makeup under my bed. Then I sat down in my beanbag chair and grabbed a maga-zine for that amazingly-cool-and-collected look. "In here, Mom."

Mom opened my door and peeked into my room. "Hi, honey. Did you have a good time at the mall?"

"Yes."

Mom looked around my bedroom. "So where are your new clothes?"

"Oh, I didn't get any after all," I said.

"Well, maybe we can go shopping together next weekend. I'll help you find something nice." Mom smiled.

"Okay," I said, but my heart sank. If we did that, she'd find out that I had spent the money. "Don't forget about your dentist appointment tomorrow—nine o'clock," she added.

"I won't," I promised.

Mom started to leave, then peeked in again. "Are you feeling okay? You're acting a little strange."

"I'm just tired."

"All right. I won't bother you anymore."

As soon as my mother left, I opened the bottom drawer of my dresser, reached underneath a pile of winter sweaters, and pulled out my diary.

Dear Diary,

I can't believe I ever liked Jake Meadows! Sure, he's cute, but he's such a little kid. As soon as Mr. Monroe stared at me, I stopped being twelve. I feel as though I've matured so much in one day.

Besides, Jake and I don't have anything in common. Mr. Monroe is gorgeous—and he loves science, too. It couldn't be more perfect! I just hope he thinks so too when he sees me in my makeup.

—R

Dr. Koury put a piece of plastic in my mouth. I bit down to hold it in place. "Does that feel okay?" she asked.

I nodded. I meant to say, "How much longer?" but it came out, "Hoh mu fwonga?" It was hard to talk with all the stuff in my mouth.

"Oh, it won't be very long now," Dr. Koury explained as she walked out of the room so she could take the X-ray. "You're almost done."

I could hardly wait to get to school. Anne had let me borrow her dark blue dress with little white squiggles all over it, since I had agreed to wash dishes on her nights for a month. (She'll only let me borrow something if I do a million of her chores.) The dress matched my favorite navy suede clogs perfectly. And my makeup was in my backpack, ready to go.

"Open up," Dr. Koury said when she came

back into the room. She reached into my mouth and pulled the little X-ray thing out. "You did a great job."

"Am I done?"

"Almost," Dr. Koury said. "I'd like you to stay here a minute. I want to talk to your mother."

"Is something wrong?"

"There's nothing to worry about. I'll be right back."

After what seemed like an hour, Dr. Koury finally came back with my mom. "Okay, Rosie," my dentist said. "You can go now."

I looked from Mom to Dr. Koury, then back to Mom. Their faces were completely blank. Whatever they'd been talking about had to be pretty terrible if they couldn't even tell me.

"So what's wrong with me?" I asked.

"Well—" Mom hesitated. "I was going to wait until after I talked to your father, but I suppose I can tell you now." She laid her hand on mine. "Dr. Koury thinks you should get braces."

What? Braces? "I don't need braces," I protested. "My teeth are straight." I smiled to emphasize my point.

"Your front teeth are very straight," Dr. Koury agreed. "But some of your teeth are crowded in the back, and you have a slight overbite."

Lucy's sad face popped into my mind. I remembered her awful headgear.

"Isn't there a way to fix my teeth besides braces?"

"I'm afraid that braces are the only way to correct your problems," Dr. Koury said.

"I won't have to wear a headgear, will I?"

"The orthodontist will decide about that," my mother said.

"Don't I get any say about this?" I asked. "I mean, this should be my decision."

"No, it shouldn't." My mother cupped my chin with her hand and grinned.

I crossed my arms over my chest. "There's no way any guy will ever look at me now," I mumbled.

"In a couple of years, you won't be able to keep the boys away," Mom said cheerfully. "You'll be thankful you have a beautiful smile." My mother gave Dr. Koury one of those looks that adults give other adults when they think you're being cute.

I walked out of the office. There was nothing cute about making me get braces. I couldn't wait two years to look beautiful. Mr. Monroe was teaching our class for just a month. I had to look beautiful now.

The secretary in Whitman's main office slid a clipboard across the counter to Mom. "Sign this, please." She pulled out a tiny pad of paper. "Name, please."

"Rosie Banton," my mother told her.

"Reason for tardiness?"

"She had a dental appointment," Mom explained.

"Who's your second-period teacher?"

"Mr. Dallas," I said.

The secretary looked at the big gray clock on the wall and wrote the time on the piece of paper. "Here you go," she said, handing me my late slip. "Just give this to your teacher when you get to class."

Mom placed her hand on my head. "I'll see you this afternoon."

I said good-bye and watched her walk out the school's double doors to the parking lot.

As soon as it was safe, I raced down the hall and into the nearest girls' bathroom. I unzipped my backpack, pulled out the bag of makeup, and placed the jars, brushes, and bottles around the edge of the sink.

I carefully smoothed the foundation with a sponge exactly the way Lenora had shown me.

Sucking in my cheeks as if I'd just eaten a lemon, I dusted my cheekbones with blush. I pushed the thoughts of braces out of my mind. Today I would look incredibly sophisticated.

I smoothed on lipstick, kissed a tissue, and looked at my new face in the mirror. *Excellent!* I thought. *Mr. Monroe won't be able to take his eyes off of me.*

I packed up my stuff and headed out into the hall. My heart practically stopped as I looked at the clock. My pass said I had gotten to school half an hour before. How could it have taken so long just to put on my makeup?

I raced to my second-period class. Taking a deep breath, I pushed the door open. All of the kids were reading silently. Trying to keep my hand from shaking, I gave my teacher the pass.

"Thank you," Mr. Dallas said, putting the pass to the side of his desk.

Phew. He didn't even notice how late I was.

"Rosie, could you come back here?" my teacher said, just as I'd made it to my desk.

A hot feeling rushed from my feet to my head. I touched my face to make sure my makeup wasn't melting off.

"What is it, Mr. Dallas?" I asked innocently when I got to his desk.

"This pass says you arrived more than half an hour ago. What have you been doing all this time?"

I bit my lower lip and studied the pass as though I hadn't seen it before. "Well," I said slowly, "I had to go to my locker. It's on the second floor."

Mr. Dallas stared at my full backpack. "Please come into the hall with me," he said sternly.

My heart thudded. If he called my parents about this, I wouldn't be allowed to go outside until I was eighteen.

As I followed Mr. Dallas into the hall, I felt a lot of kids staring at me. Out of the corner of my eye, I could see the sneer on Shannon's perfect face. So I turned to give her my most serious glare. Shannon's mouth dropped open.

I wanted to laugh. Shannon and I shot each other dirty looks all the time. During the first couple weeks of school, I'd actually been a part of her crowd, hanging out with her at the Pop Stop and eating at her lunch table. Then Shannon started bad-mouthing Amy and Heather. So I told her off in front of the entire lunchroom. Ever since then we've been enemies.

There was one big difference between today and all the other times, though. This time, I was wearing makeup—and Shannon had given me just the reaction I had hoped for.

Mr. Dallas shut the door behind us. "Okay, Rosie—out with it," he said. "What's going on?"

"Um…would you believe it if I told you that the office secretary wrote down the wrong time?"

"I don't think so."

"All right," I said in a resigned tone. "The truth is I didn't finish my homework last night, so I went to the library and did it when I got here today." I reached into my backpack and pulled out my completed homework.

Mr. Dallas pursed his lips. "Not bad, Rosie. That's the best excuse I've heard all year." He took the notebook paper from my hand. "You can go back in and read with the rest of the class."

Not bad at all, I thought. *Shannon's bug-eyed over how amazing I look in makeup* and *I'm not in trouble.*

If things were working out this well already, I was more excited than ever for sixth period—and Mr. Monroe.

Chapter 5

"When is he going to come out of there?" I whispered to Amy and Heather at the beginning of sixth period. Mr. Monroe was talking with Mr. Norris in the equipment storage room.

"Let them take their time," Amy said. "I'm in no hurry."

"Well *I* am." I was certain I'd spontaneously combust if I had to wait one more second to see Mr. Monroe's gorgeous eyes.

"I'll be right back," I told my friends. I peeked into the storage room. Mr. Norris held a piece of paper in front of Mr. Monroe and pointed to the shelves around them. Mr. Monroe wrinkled his forehead and nodded.

He's even more handsome when he's concentrating, I thought.

"Does all of this make sense, Jason?" Mr. Norris said.

Jason. His name is Jason, I repeated to myself. Jason was the most perfect name in the world—almost as perfect as the guy.

"Jason and Rosie Monroe," I whispered.

"What was that, Miss Banton?" Mr. Norris asked.

I snapped out of my thoughts and saw my two science teachers staring at me. "I—I—was just checking to see if you needed any help."

"Not now, but thank you." Mr. Norris turned to Jason. "If you ever need anything, you can always count on Rosie to help you."

"That's good to know," Jason said. When he smiled, his eyebrows went up a tiny bit. Was he sending me one of those secret signals that guys send girls? There was a whole article about it in the July issue of *Contemporary Teen.* It was called body language. I was sure that raised eyebrows meant something good.

My feet felt as if they were barely touching the floor as I hurried back to my desk.

"Gee, Rosie," Glen Benedict said when I sat down again. "You look really pretty!"

"Thanks, Glen."

Heather leaned forward. "Did she just say 'Thanks, Glen'? What happened to 'Buzz off, Glen'?" she whispered to Amy.

"I think we'd better check her temperature," Amy answered urgently. "She might be sick." She and Heather giggled.

"I'm not sick," I said, grinning mischievously. "I'm just in a very good mood."

"Here they come," Heather whispered. I sat up straight in my chair.

"Let's get started," Jason announced as Mr. Norris carried a pile of papers to an empty table in the back of the room. "In addition to your regular lessons, I'll be working with you on your science projects for the Whitman seventh-grade science fair. You'll be required to come up with a theme and put together a special display. The projects will be graded and, if you decide to enter, judged at the fair. Any questions?"

I raised my hand. "How will the projects be judged?"

"Good question, Rosie," Jason said, smiling. "Three judges will evaluate your work and award ribbons based on how they compare to the others. Twenty-five students will receive honorable mentions. One student each will be given second and third place. And the student who finishes in first place will go to the county finals."

I grew excited and nervous at the same time.

There were more than two hundred seventh graders, and most of them would probably compete in the science fair. But my biggest competition was sitting right behind me— Heather. She was a super-brain and got straight A's. I did as well as she did in science, but, unlike me, Heather didn't have to work very hard.

One reason I hated the idea of competing with Heather was that she'd been through a lot lately. Her dad died about a year ago in a car crash. Then her mom had to sell the farm where Heather grew up. And a little while ago, she got a letter from her birth mother saying she wanted to meet her. (That's when Amy and I found out that she was adopted.) Heather decided to meet her birth mother, and that turned out okay. Still, I knew that Heather had had a tough time dealing with all of this.

"In addition," Jason continued, "the first-place ribbon winners from all five junior high schools in the area will be part of the science buddy program at Central Virginia Tech. You'll work with me and four other science majors in the university's lab."

"Awesome," Glen said.

No way, Glen, I thought. *"Awesome" doesn't*

begin to describe how amazing it would be to work side-by-side with Jason.

"We'll continue with your regular lessons during class, but I'll be available after school every day if you'd like to work on your projects here. All of the rules are listed on this handout," Jason explained as he walked over to my table with the stack of papers. "Would you please hand these out for me, Rosie?"

"Uh huh," I said eagerly. As I took the papers from him, our hands touched. A weird shiver ran down my spine. Had Jason felt it too?

"Mr. Norris usually just gives each row a few handouts," Aaron Greenberg called out. "The first person takes one and passes the rest back."

"I think it'll be all right if Rosie helps me out this time." Jason's eyes glistened as he spoke. My palms were so sweaty I was sure they'd wilt the papers. There was no doubt about it: Jason had actually noticed me.

Dear Diary,
    I've never felt so wonderful in my entire life. It was completely different when I liked other guys. I didn't think about them constantly, the way I do with Jason. I wasn't sure at first, but

now I know there's only one reason I feel so fantastic all the time. I'm in love!

That's why I have to make sure that Jason understands how perfect we are for each other. I absolutely have to win the science fair and be his science buddy.

I've already picked my topic: garbage and recycling. It shows how much I care about the world. That should really impress Jason.

I feel pretty rotten about wanting to beat Heather. But she's already been in a special science program at her old school. Someone else should get a turn. Me.

-R

"Yvonne called today," my mother announced at dinner that night.

"Is she coming home?" I asked excitedly.

"She didn't say anything about that. She wanted to tell me where she's going to donate her money."

The money! In all of the excitement, I'd forgotten about it.

"So," Anne said. "What's Yvonne doing with her money?"

"She's sending it to an organization that feeds starving people in Africa," Mom explained.

"That's nice," Nanna commented.

Anne reached for the bowl of rice. "I'm contributing mine to the Englewood Symphony Orchestra," she told everyone proudly.

"Have you decided what you're going to do with yours yet?" Dad asked me.

"No, I'm still thinking," I mumbled, praying that the phone would ring or that an elephant would run through the dining room so that they wouldn't ask any more questions. I couldn't tell them I'd spent all the money *and* broken one of their biggest rules by wearing makeup. Once the environment club community project was a huge success and we'd saved part of the rain forest, I was sure they'd figure that I'd added my donation money to the club's money.

"Well, there's no reason to rush," Mom said. "I'm very proud of my daughters for what they're doing." She put a big pot in front of me. "Have some more stew. You're eating like a bird tonight."

I pushed my dinner around on my plate. "I'm

not really hungry." Somehow Mom's sweetness made me feel even worse.

"You're not worried about getting braces, are you?" my mother asked.

"No, I had forgotten all about that," I said, dropping my fork. It was as though my mother had sensors that told her exactly what I didn't want to talk about.

"I've made an orthodontist appointment for you on Friday," my mother went on.

"*This* Friday? Can't we wait...even a month?"

"The sooner you do it, the less time you'll spend worrying about it," my father said.

Anne made a clicking sound with her tongue. "I'm glad I didn't have to get braces. I'd hate to have all that metal in my mouth."

"Rosie will be even prettier in braces," Nanna told my sister cheerfully.

"If Rosie doesn't get her teeth straightened now, it could lead to problems later," Dad added. "We're not just doing this for her looks."

"Anyway, I hope you picked a good ortho-dontist," Anne said skeptically. "I know a girl whose teeth looked just fine until she went to a quack doctor to get braces. She ended up with buck teeth." She made a face like a beaver.

"You're such a creep!" I shouted, getting up

from the table. "I can't stand you!"

"Don't forget you have to do the dishes for me tonight," Anne called after me as I ran to my room.

I knew Anne was lying about her friend, but she was right about all of the metal. Who cared about good teeth if you had to look horrible to get that way?

I grabbed the phone from the hall and took it back to my bedroom, then dialed Yvonne's phone number at college.

"Hello?" Yvonne answered.

"Hi, Yvonne."

"Hey, Rosie! What's up?"

"Out of all the sisters in the world, why did I have to get stuck with Anne?"

"Are you guys fighting about clothes again?"

"I wish," I said glumly. "It's way worse than that. And this time it's not completely her fault. It's a conspiracy."

"By whom?"

"Well, my dentist, for one. She says I need braces."

"Oh, yeah. Mom told me about that when I called today."

I sighed. "This is a nightmare. The guys will think I'm a major geek."

"Even if some guys don't like them, the *mature* ones will see how beautiful you are no matter what. My roommate has braces, and guys ask her out all the time."

"Really?"

Yvonne giggled. "Trust me. The phone never stops ringing."

As usual, Yvonne had said the perfect thing to make me feel better. I knew she really meant it; she wasn't just trying to cheer me up. And she was right. After all, I wasn't interested in impressing a bunch of immature junior high school guys. There was only one person I wanted to impress—and he was practically a college graduate.

"And if I show them how special I am on the inside, I'll seem twice as pretty on the outside," I said, quoting something my father had told us about a million times.

"That's the Banton spirit," Yvonne said. "So when is your orthodontist appointment?"

"Friday. I won't get my braces, though. It's just for tests and stuff."

"How about if I come home this weekend? We can go to the candy store and pig out on peanut brittle and taffy."

I giggled at the thought of one last feast on

all the stuff I wouldn't be able to eat once I got my braces. "And Fruit Goos," I added. "Can you pick me up at school? I want you to meet my science teacher."

"Sure. I'd like to meet Mr. Norris."

"Not him. We have a student teacher from Central Virginia Tech."

"Really? That's one of the best science schools in the country."

"I know." I reached for a pillow from my bed and clutched it against my heart. "Mr. Monroe is really great too."

For now, that was all I could tell Yvonne about Jason. I wanted to wait for the right moment to reveal all of my deepest feelings. I wanted to tell her in person, after I found out what she thought of him. I could hardly wait until Friday.

Chapter 6

As Mom filled out forms in the orthodontist's waiting room on Friday morning, I tried to think about what Yvonne had said about mature guys. Instead I kept remembering what Anne had said about a mouth full of metal.

"Is anyone sitting here?" I heard a voice beside me. When I glanced up, a girl who looked a little older than me was pointing to the seat next to me. She had short reddish brown hair and round wire glasses. She was wearing red leggings, black cowboy boots, and an oversized white shirt.

"No, sit down," I told her.

"This must be your first time here," the girl said.

"How'd you know?"

"Well, you don't have braces—and you look pretty nervous."

I looked at my fingernails, which I'd been biting. "I guess I'm not too thrilled about getting braces."

"I know how you feel. I got mine when I was twelve. Most of my friends had already gotten theirs off."

"You have braces?" I asked. "All I see is a little wire."

"They're cosmetic. They cost more than the regular ones, but they're worth it. My parents didn't want me to look like a geek."

"Rosie Banton," called a woman in a pink shirt and white pants.

My mother stood up and tapped me on the shoulder. "That's us."

"Hi, Linda," the girl said to the woman in the pink shirt.

The woman looked at her and smiled. "Hi, Cassandra. How is everything?"

"Great!" Then Cassandra turned to me. "Maybe I'll see you later."

"Uh huh. Thanks." I felt much better as I followed my mother and Linda down the hall. Cassandra seemed really cool and nice. But the best part about meeting her was that now I knew I didn't have to have a metal mouth.

"There are several types of braces that you can get," the orthodontist, Dr. Price, explained after he had examined me. He handed my mother and me a picture.

"This girl doesn't have braces," I said, looking at the photograph. Unlike Cassandra, the girl in the picture didn't even have a wire.

Dr. Price chuckled. "Actually, her braces are on the back of her teeth. They're called lingual braces."

These were even better than Cassandra's.

"That's what I want," I said excitedly.

"Would these be good for Rosie?" Mom asked.

"The lingual braces don't show the way standard braces do. Unfortunately, they hurt more than the other kinds because they tend to cut your tongue. And they have to be worn twice as long as the ones that go on the front of your teeth."

"Oh," I said as I handed the photograph back to my orthodontist. Just hearing about the lingual braces made my tongue hurt. And I didn't want to wear braces any longer than I had to.

"Do you have ones that don't hurt and don't show?"

Dr. Price gave us another picture. The braces were like Cassandra's. "I can hardly see these," I said. "Are they really painful?"

"Not really. But ceramic brackets do have one big drawback. They're extremely well bonded to the teeth, which makes them hard to remove."

"You mean I might have to wear them forever?"

Dr. Price laughed and shook his head. "Sometimes when they're removed, the enamel from your tooth comes off too. You need enamel to keep your teeth strong and healthy. Once it's gone, it can't be replaced naturally."

"Can't you just be careful when you take them off?"

"I'm afraid I don't always have control over it. It's the nature of the braces."

"I don't care. I still want these. I'm willing to take a chance."

"What do you recommend?" my mother asked the orthodontist.

"Most of my patients wear these." He handed us another photo. The smiling mouth had braces just like Lucy's.

"I'd rather get the ones you can't see," I told them.

"Well, I think you should get these," Mom said. "It's no use having expensive braces if they're just going to damage your teeth. Besides, it will only be for about two years."

"Two years! I can't wear metal braces until I'm fourteen!"

My mother let out a long sigh. "How often do the ceramic braces cause damage?" she asked the orthodontist.

"Not very often, really," Dr. Price said. "But if you're concerned, there is one other solution. I could put ceramic brackets on the top six front teeth and metal on the others. People will hardly ever see the metal brackets. And there's even less of a chance of damage."

I really wanted to get braces just like Cassandra's. I thought about insisting until my mother gave in. But if I complained too much, I'd end up with huge silver railroad tracks on every tooth.

"I guess I'm willing to compromise if you are," I told my mother.

"Well, I suppose that would be all right," my mother agreed.

"I'll have my receptionist set up an appointment for you to get your braces," Dr. Price said cheerfully.

Before lunch that afternoon, I checked out my makeup in the mirror inside my locker. "Do you think I need more lipstick?" I asked Amy and Heather.

Amy shook her head. "It'll all come off when you eat anyway."

"I guess you're right. I hate looking at food that has lipstick smeared all over it."

Heather looked at all of the bottles and compacts sitting on my locker shelf. "Do your books fit in here anymore?" she asked.

"Ha ha," I said. "I have to keep all my makeup here so my parents don't find out about it. I've worn it every day this week, and they're still clueless."

"I guess if I started wearing makeup, I'd have to keep it in my locker, too," Heather said.

Amy shook her head. "Please don't do that. If both of you get caught, I won't have anyone to go to the Pop Stop with." We all laughed. Amy didn't have anything to worry about. Heather's mom can be as strict as my parents, but, unlike me, Heather doesn't sneak around behind her mother's back.

The three of us headed downstairs to the cafeteria.

"Amy and I figured we'd come to your house at seven forty-five for our sleepover tonight," Heather said. "That way, we'll have enough time to make popcorn before *One Big Family*." *One Big Family* is a sitcom about a family with eleven kids. I used to have a major crush on Donny Davenport, who plays the oldest brother, Sam.

"I'm kind of tired of *One Big Family*," I said. "I asked Yvonne to take us bowling instead."

"Are you kidding?" Amy asked. "It's your favorite show!"

"What about Donny Davenport?" Heather added.

"He's really not my type."

"Since when?" Amy asked suspiciously.

"Since Jason, of course." I scratched my face.

"What's wrong with your cheek?" Heather asked.

"What do you mean?" I asked.

"You keep scratching it."

"It's probably just a nervous reaction."

"What are you nervous about?" Amy wondered.

"Well, for one thing, I'm scared my parents

are getting suspicious about the donation money. *And* I'm getting my braces *next week*." I sighed. "What is Jason going to think?"

"If he's as wonderful as you think he is, he'll like you with or without the braces," Heather assured me.

"That's what Yvonne said, too."

"You told her about Mr. Monroe?" Amy asked.

"Well, not exactly. I want to see what she thinks of him first."

"I guess our opinion isn't good enough!" Heather said, pretending to be offended.

"That's not it. I already know that you guys think I should forget about him."

"It just seems kind of…strange," Amy said hesitantly. "I mean, he's our teacher."

"Only for three more weeks. Then he'll go back to being a regular student—just like us."

"Not for long. He's going to graduate from college this year," Heather reminded me. "We'll still be in junior high school."

"Hmmm, dating a college graduate," I mused. "I kind of like the sound of that."

Chapter 7

"All this book talks about is how you should bring your own canvas bags to the grocery," I told Amy as I shut my book and slid it to the edge of the science table after school on Friday. "Maybe I should choose another topic." I was all for eliminating inorganic waste, but I wanted my science project to be more complex—more scientific.

Amy drew a straight line with a Magic Marker. Her science fair project was a comparison of the standing broad jump and the running long jump. "I think recycling is a good topic," she said. "I bet you'll figure out something."

"But Heather's getting way ahead of me."

Amy stopped coloring and looked up. "You shouldn't compare yourself to Heather. She's a total brain."

"Yeah, but science is my best subject, and I'm totally stuck."

"Maybe you should ask Mr. Monroe for help," Amy suggested.

"Are you kidding? And let him know I'm having trouble?"

"He wouldn't care. He's helping everyone."

"I know, but he might think I'm not very good in science."

Still, I wished there was some way to get Jason's attention without looking like a dummy. For the past week, I had dreamed about the moment when I would show him my project. *This is the most incredible science project I've seen in my life*, Jason would say. Then he'd pull me close and look at me with his fabulous eyes. I'd be smiling, beaming with joy. *And you're the most incredible girl I've ever known. Your braces make you even more beautiful.*

That was one version. In the other one, Jason sees my braces, screams "You're hideous!" and runs out of the room.

Whether or not Jason liked my braces, I knew he definitely wouldn't call my science project "incredible" if he saw it now.

"Help!" a familiar voice squeaked, snapping me out of my thoughts. A pile of books with legs was staggering into the science room.

"Heather!" I shouted as Amy and I jumped out of our seats and rushed over to carry some of the books.

"What are all of these for?" Amy asked.

"My project. They've all got information about how dogs hear," she explained excitedly.

"All of these books are about dogs' ears?" I asked.

Heather nodded. "Uh huh—and human ears. I can't believe how lucky I am."

"Neither can I," I mumbled as we put the books on the table. "Have you figured out what you're going to do yet?"

"I'm going to make a papier-mâché model of a human ear and a dog's ear," Heather said excitedly. "Then I'll show what's the same and what's different about each one."

"That'll be really cool," Amy told her.

"Yeah," I said, putting my head down on the table. "Real cool." How was I going to beat her?

"Hello, little sis." I lifted my head back up when I heard Yvonne's voice. With her curly black hair falling loosely around her face, she looked as pretty as ever.

I ran to the door and gave her a huge hug. "I'm so glad you're here."

"I was so excited to see you that I haven't even been home yet. Are you ready to go?"

"You have to meet Mr. Monroe first, remember? He's back in the storage room. And Heather." I walked her over to the table to introduce her to my new friend.

"I'm so glad to meet you," Yvonne told Heather. "Rosie talks about you all the time."

Heather's round cheeks turned bright pink. "Thanks. It's nice to meet you, too."

"Hey, Amy," Yvonne said. "How's Whitman's track star?"

"Sore. We had a killer workout yesterday."

I grabbed Yvonne's arm and led her to the storage room. Suddenly, my nerves went into high gear. Introducing Jason to my favorite sister made my heart pound. "Yvonne, this is Mr. Monroe, our student teacher. Mr. Monroe, this is my sister, Yvonne."

Yvonne stuck her hand out to Jason. "Hi. Nice to meet you."

Jason shook her hand. "Hello. You can't be going to school here, though," he said, flashing one of his spectacular smiles.

Yvonne laughed. "Actually, I'm just visiting from college. I'm afraid I haven't been fulfilling my sisterly duties very well lately, so I came back home for the weekend to make up for it."

"From where?"

"Blue Ridge State. I'm a freshman there."

"Really? They have some great programs. What's your major?" Jason asked.

"I'm not sure yet. Maybe history or sociology," Yvonne told him.

"Not a science field?"

"No way. Rosie's the scientist in our family," Yvonne said, putting her arm around me. "Well, we'd better get going."

"See you on Monday, Mr. Monroe," I said as we walked out the door.

"It was nice to meet you," Yvonne called back to Jason.

Jason waved. "You, too."

Once we'd picked up Amy and Heather and walked out into the hall, Yvonne looked at me suspiciously. "Are you wearing makeup?"

"Uh huh. Do you like it?"

"Mom and Dad didn't let me wear makeup until I was fourteen."

"Well, they're not exactly *letting* me. They don't even know I have makeup. I have to wash it all off before I go home. You won't tell on me, will you?" I asked.

"Of course not, Rosie," she said, laughing.

"What kind of a sister do you think I am?"

"I guess I've just gotten used to Anne," I said.

Yvonne giggled. "Be careful, though. Mom and Dad have ways of finding out things."

I stopped in front of the girls' bathroom. "I'll wash my face right now."

"I'm going to go ahead. I need to get some books out of my locker," Amy said.

"Me too," Heather added.

"Okay. We'll meet you out by the main entrance," I told them as Yvonne and I went into the girls' room. I unscrewed the lid of my cleansing cream and smeared it all over my face.

"Why didn't you tell me that your teacher is so good-looking?" Yvonne asked, leaning against the sink next to me.

"Do you really think so?" I asked.

"I probably would have done a lot better in science if I'd had a teacher like him," she said, chuckling.

Yay, I thought with relief. *I knew that Yvonne would think he's cute too. Now she'll definitely get into helping me make Jason notice me.* "Um, actually, there's something I've been waiting to tell you." I took a deep breath. "I'm totally—"

"I practically begged him to let Jake come, but Mr. Schneider said no eighth graders were allowed at the seventh-grade dance," Shannon said loudly as she and her friend Wendy walked into the bathroom.

I glared at them. Leave it to Shannon to make her entrance at the worst possible moment.

Shannon looked at me as though she'd just seen a ghost.

Then she turned to Wendy, and both of them broke into hysterical laughter. *What's so funny?* I wondered as I watched them walk to the other end of the wall.

That's when I saw my face, still smeared with cream, in the mirror. *How embarrassing!* I bent over and frantically grabbed a tissue out of my makeup bag.

"What did you want to tell me?" Yvonne asked eagerly.

"Oh, nothing," I said as I wiped every bit of cream off my face. "I'll tell you later. Let's get out of here."

It could have been worse, I thought as I rushed out of the bathroom. *Shannon could have overheard my confession.*

As much as I wanted to confide in my sister, my news was way too important to blab in the middle of school—or with anyone nearby.

Dear Diary,

It's so excellent having Yvonne here. Amy and Heather don't get why I love Jason, but Yvonne sees how great he is.

Maybe Jason's the man I'm going to marry!

I want to have the most perfect wedding ever. Yvonne will be my maid of honor. Amy and Heather will be bridesmaids, of course. I'm going to design all of the dresses. Theirs will be purple. Mine is going to be all white lace with real pearls stitched in.

Unfortunately, I haven't had a chance to tell Yvonne about Jason yet. Someone is always around. I can hardly keep it in anymore. But I guess I'll just have to. That's okay, though. Now that I know Jason has Yvonne's seal of approval, there's no stopping me.

-R

Chapter 8

"Rise and shine, sleepyheads!" Yvonne shouted.

"What time is it?" I mumbled, turning over in my sleeping bag.

"Seven-thirty," Yvonne answered. "Just an hour to get ready before the environment club cleanup."

Heather and I sat up groggily. Amy yawned and rolled over. After we got back from bowling the night before, Yvonne was so tired that she went straight to bed. But Amy, Heather, and I had important stuff to talk about—like how great Yvonne is, how spectacular Jason is, and how I was ever going to come up with all the money I was supposed to donate before my parents found out I'd spent most of it on makeup. By the time we conked out at three A.M., we still hadn't come up with a solution to my money problem.

Yvonne grinned at us. "How late did you guys stay up?"

"Don't ask," Heather said, flopping back on her pillow. "It makes me tired just thinking about it."

I stretched my arms over my head. "I'll make breakfast."

"Is it okay if I take a shower?" Heather asked. "That might help me wake up."

"You can use the bathroom in the hall," Yvonne told her as she walked out of the room. "I'll use the one downstairs."

I looked over at Amy, who had fallen back to sleep in record time. "What are we going to do about her?" I asked, crawling out of my sleeping bag.

"We might as well let her sleep a little bit longer," Heather said. "We'd need a bulldozer to get her up now anyway." She pulled a fluffy pink towel out of her overnight sack and left to take her shower.

I grabbed my purple robe from its hanger and looked at my face in the mirror on my closet door.

"Aaaaaa!" I screamed.

Amy sprang up out of her mummy bag. "What's wrong?"

"Is everything all right?" Heather asked breathlessly as she bounded in from the hallway.

"Look at my face!" I shrieked, pointing to the bumps that had invaded my right cheek during the night.

Amy curled her lip and leaned closer. "What is it?"

"It looks like a rash," Heather said.

Yvonne raced into my room, clutching the front of her robe. She had a shower cap on her head. "What's going on? Who screamed?"

"Rosie has a rash on her face," Amy told her.

"Let me see," Yvonne said.

I turned my head to give her a better look. "Do you think it will leave a scar?"

Yvonne shook her head. "It really isn't that bad."

I examined the bumpy patch in the mirror again. How could she say it wasn't that bad? Braces might be one thing, but there was no way that anyone, mature or not, would think this was beautiful. "Listen," I said urgently, "we can get to the school early, and I'll cover it up with makeup before the other kids get there."

"I don't think makeup is such a good idea," Yvonne said. "That's probably how you got the rash in the first place. Your skin might be too sensitive."

"But I can't go out looking like this!" With my luck, I'd run into Shannon again. She'd never stop laughing.

"I'm sure Dad can give you something to clear it up," Yvonne told me. He's a doctor and keeps different kinds of medicine at home.

"I can't tell Dad," I said. "He'll punish me for wearing makeup."

Yvonne wrapped her arms around my shoulders. "Relax. We don't have to tell him how you got the rash."

I hung my head. "Even if Dad has something, the bumps won't be gone before the cleanup. Maybe you guys should go without me."

"You have to go, Rosie," Amy said. "You're president of the club. And the cleanup was your idea."

Amy was right. I owed it to the club to be there—especially after spending the money I'd promised to donate. And all I had to show for it was an expensive rash and a big pile of useless makeup.

"I have an idea," Yvonne said confidently. "Come with me." The three of us followed her down the hall to her bedroom.

Yvonne got down on her knees and peeked under her bed. Dust bunnies flew through the air as she pulled out a broken-down suitcase, a pair of old roller skates, and a stuffed hippo with one eye missing.

"I know it's here somewhere," Yvonne muttered.

What could Yvonne possibly have under her bed that was going to magically transform me?

"Here it is!" Yvonne shouted triumphantly as she held out a floppy blue polka-dot hat that she had worn to the pool over the summer. The huge rim kept the sun out of her eyes.

Yvonne planted the hat on my head and pulled it down over my ears so that it practically covered my face. "People will be so busy looking at your hat that they won't even notice your cheek."

"Are you sure it doesn't look stupid?" I asked, lifting the edge.

Yvonne took a gold pin out of her jewelry box and pinned the rim up in the front. The sides still covered my cheeks pretty well. "With a pair of overalls, it'll be perfect for the cleanup."

When it came to fashion, I trusted my sister more than anyone else in the world.

"What are we waiting for then?" I said, smiling. "Let's get ready!"

"Thanks for giving us all of this stuff, Mom," Amy said as we lugged a huge box of aluminum cans out of the door of Carol's Catering, the gourmet food shop that Mrs. Spinosa, Amy's mom, opened a couple of years ago in downtown Englewood.

Mrs. Spinosa wiped her hands on her white apron. "I should be thanking you," she told us. "My assistant was out sick this week. I've been so busy that I couldn't get down to the recycling center."

"We'd better put this stuff in the van and go meet everyone else there," I told Heather and Amy. "We don't want to be late again."

By the time we had eaten breakfast, gotten dressed, put Dad's medicine on my rash, and made it to the Whitman Junior High parking lot, everyone else had been waiting for us. The whole environment club showed up. Some of them had brought friends and brothers and sisters. And five parents had offered to drive kids around to collect recyclables. Including Yvonne, Amy, and Heather, there were twenty-two people.

Everyone divided up into groups so that practically every neighborhood in Englewood was covered. The four of us volunteered to clean up the Green, which is a park in the middle of Englewood.

After we had finished searching for cans and bottles in the bushes at the Green, we hit the shops and offices on the streets around it. If the other kids had collected half as much as we did, the club wouldn't even need the money I had promised to donate.

When we arrived at the recycling center, Jeff Pollack and Matt Petursson, two club members, were unloading some large trash cans from the back of Mrs. Pollack's pickup truck.

"Wow!" Amy said. "You got even more than we did."

"Some people had been saving stuff for weeks," Matt told us. "One man had cans and bottles all over his garage. His car didn't even fit."

"This is incredible!" I said. "Let's start unloading everything and find out how much money we made."

As we emptied the recyclables from the van, other kids arrived and began unloading their bins, buckets, and garbage bags.

"Look at all the stuff we got!" Monica Sandborn, the vice-president of the club, said to me proudly.

I silently cheered. The community project was turning out even better than I had hoped.

"We'd like to find out how much money we can get for all of this," I told a tall man standing nearby.

"Kyle! Joe!" the tall man shouted. "Come help me with this." Two men walked over and began separating the recyclables. When all of the glass was on the scale, the tall man wrote something. They did the same thing with the aluminum.

The man looked at his piece of paper. "You kids did a great job. You've earned sixty-seven dollars."

"*Sixty-seven dollars?* That's all?" Monica asked.

All this stuff had to be worth more than that. "Could you please weigh it again?" I asked.

"That number seems just right to me," the man said. "There are nearly thirty cans in a pound of aluminum. We pay twenty-two cents per pound."

"Isn't the glass worth more?" I asked hopefully.

"Well, a glass bottle weighs more than an aluminum can," the man explained, "but they're only worth a penny a pound."

The club members began to mumble and groan.

"Listen, you guys," Monica announced. "We'll still be able to buy an acre of rain forest—thanks to Rosie's contribution!"

"Oh, yeah, that's right," Jeff said, brightening.

"Let's hear it for Rosie!" Carrie Jacobs yelled.

The other kids cheered.

"Shouldn't you tell them the truth?" Amy whispered in my ear.

"I'm going to get myself out of this mess," I told her. "Somehow." I looked at all of the happy faces around me. I couldn't let everyone down.

"By the way," I said to Amy as we all headed back to the cars. "How did Simon's Cub Scout troop collect so much more than us?"

Amy's face turned pink. "I guess I kind of forgot the fact that they collected stuff for six weeks."

"Oh, great," I groaned.

Heather put her hand on my shoulder. "Well, at least we learned something about recycling today," she said. "You have to drink more than twenty six-packs of soda to get a dollar's worth of aluminum."

"That's it!" I shouted.

"Well, I don't really think that we should drink all that soda."

"No, I mean the other part. We really did learn something about recycling today. Maybe the people here can help me with my science project."

"Why don't we go ask them?" Amy said.

We turned around and raced back to the building. The tall man who had helped us before was still waiting outside. "Excuse me," I said. "Could you show me how this stuff is turned into new things?"

"Well, we don't actually recycle here," he explained. "We send everything to a plant to be cleaned and prepared for the manufacturers. But I can show you how we separate the materials before we send them away."

"Okay," I said.

First, the man gave us hard hats and goggles to wear. Then, we followed him through a door that said AUTHORIZED PERSONNEL ONLY and into a huge room with vats of water, conveyor belts, and large magnets. A pile of garbage traveled from one station to the next. At each step, different items were removed from the pile.

"The things that get taken out of the batch are called contaminants," the man yelled over all over the activity in the room. "Those are the things that can't be recycled or need to be recycled separately."

"How do the machines know what to take out?" Heather asked.

"It's all based on the physical properties of each item."

"You mean what they're made of?" I asked.

"Right. Steel and plastic are very different materials. When you drop plastic in water, it floats. We remove all of the plastic by dumping everything in a vat of water. But there are other contaminants we have to get rid of, so we have to find another way to separate materials like steel. For that, we just use a magnet to pull it out of the pile of aluminum."

"What happens to the glass?" Heather asked.

"That's broken up into tiny pieces called cullet," the man explained. "I can give you some brochures that'll tell you more about what goes on at a recycling plant."

"That would be great!" I told him enthusiastically. *I might really win the science fair,* I thought. The thought of taking the blue ribbon—and of working with Jason in his college lab—practically made all of my troubles disappear.

I grabbed one copy of everything, and we all went back to the van. "This is really going to help me with my science fair project," I said.

Yvonne started the engine. "I can't wait till the fair."

"You're really going to come home again just to see my science fair project?"

"I wouldn't miss it. Now let's go home and clean up. Mom said she'd treat us all to pizza!"

"Awesome!" I shouted.

Chapter 9

Dear Diary,

If I have to spend another minute away from Jason, I think I'll die! I can't get him out of my head. Having Yvonne around made it almost bearable, but she left to go back to college a little while ago. I still haven't told her about Jason and me. Every time I tried, Anne had to come along and butt in. I can't tell Yvonne over the phone. Besides, I want to see the look on her face. I guess I have to wait till she comes back for the science fair. (Maybe I'll have even bigger news to tell her by then!)

-R

P.S. The stuff that Dad gave me for the rash was really good. The bumps are practically all gone. And Mom forgot all about shopping for clothes with the money I no longer have. Phew!

At the end of school on Monday, I pulled the rolled-up posters I'd made for the science fair out of my locker. After Yvonne left, I'd spent the rest of Sunday cutting out pictures from the recycling pamphlets. Then I glued everything to poster board and drew huge arrows from one picture to another to show what happens to a can or bottle before it's recycled. I couldn't wait to get to the science room—and Jason. *I just hope he likes them!* I prayed.

"What's that?" I heard Heather ask.

"Oh, hi! It's the stuff I did for my science fair project yesterday. Did you work on yours?"

Heather nodded and started dialing her locker combination. "I finished the papier-mâché human ear. It came out perfect—after about ten tries. I put it in the storage room before school today so it wouldn't get ruined."

"That's great!" I tried to sound enthusiastic.

"I'll have to show you tomorrow," Heather

told me. "I've got band practice this afternoon."

"Let us see yours," Amy said to me.

"Um…they're not ready yet," I lied. Showing my posters to Amy was one thing, but I didn't want Heather to see my work before I'd seen hers.

Amy shrugged. "I've got to get to the locker room anyway for track practice."

"Oh, my gosh! If you guys aren't working after school, I might actually get to be alone in the science room with Jason. I hope no one else shows up." My heart pounded faster.

Heather picked up her sax case. "Don't miss us too much."

"No offense." I smiled and slammed my locker. "I'll see you guys later."

I practically floated down the stairs toward the science room. Ever since the first day I saw Jason, I'd imagined having him all to myself. Today could be the day my fantasy would come true. First, we'd talk about science. He'd be so fascinated by my scientific mind that he'd want to know more—personal stuff. Then he'd realize what I've known the whole time: We were meant to be together. Age doesn't matter, and there wasn't much point in holding out any longer.

Could I take you out to dinner, Rosie? I imagined Jason's smooth, deep voice.

I'd love that, I'd say in a sophisticated tone. And we'd walk out of the room, holding hands.

The science classroom, it turned out, was empty. *Well, at least it's not full of other kids. I just hope Jason gets here soon.*

I rolled the rubber band off my posters and laid them out on my regular table; then I went back to the storage room. I couldn't wait to start on the next part of my project—a demonstration of how contaminants are separated from recyclables. I hoped it would be even better than Heather's papier-mâché ears.

Then again, Heather *had* been working pretty hard on her ears. I wouldn't know how we compared until I actually saw her project.

Maybe I should check, just in case. I looked into the classroom to make sure the coast was still clear, then searched the shelves. A white sheet disguised some kind of lumpy mass on the bottom shelf.

That's got to be it! I slowly lifted a corner of the white sheet. I could see only a small part of the ear. I pulled the sheet off and lifted the model off the shelf.

Heather was right—the model was perfect.

She had painted it in bright colors and stuck on little tags that named practically every part of the ear.

I'd seen a lot of other projects, but none were nearly this good—not counting mine, that is. The way things looked at this point, the science fair could go to either one of us.

No matter what, I couldn't let Heather beat me. I had to be Jason's science buddy. No one—not even one of my best friends—could stand in my way.

"Rosie?" Jason said behind me.

The sound of his voice startled me, and Heather's model slipped out of my hands. "Oh, no!" I shouted as the ear fell. I held my breath, waiting for it to smash to the floor. Fortunately, I had left the sheet that covered the model wadded up on the floor. The ear landed safely on the bunched-up fabric.

"That was lucky," Jason said behind me.

"You're telling *me*," I said, finally letting out my breath. "I'd better put this back." As I looked into Jason's eyes, my whole body felt like mush. We were actually alone, face to face.

"I guess we should just give these to Heather to glue back on," Jason said, bending over. My heart sank as I looked down at the spot where he was kneeling. Some of Heather's little tags were scattered on the floor at my feet.

I quickly put the ear on the floor beside me and scrambled to pick up the little white pieces of paper. "Heather's going to be so mad at me."

"I'm sure she'll understand," Jason said calmly. "You two are good friends."

He was right. Heather would know it was an accident. What she didn't know was how determined I was to beat her.

"This is my fault," I said as I picked up the tags. "Heather shouldn't have to fix something that I messed up."

As Jason put his hand on my shoulder, a warm feeling washed over me. *Is he sending me a signal?* I wondered. *Should I send some kind of signal back?*

"If it'll make you feel better," he said, "I'll get some glue, and we can put the tags back on."

"Do you know where they go?"

Jason reached up and took an anatomy book off the bookshelf. "This should tell us."

Why was Jason going to so much trouble for me? Most of my teachers probably would have lectured me about snooping and told Heather what I did. But Jason actually wanted to help me. Would he have done this for just anybody—or was he falling in love with me too?

Jason walked into the classroom holding the tiny tags in one hand and the huge science book in the other. I followed behind him with the papier-mâché ear. We put everything on a table by the door.

"I think Mr. Norris has some glue in his drawer," Jason said, walking toward the teacher's desk. When he saw my posters, he stopped. "Is this your project?"

"Um, yes," I responded nervously. "Part of it."

"It's terrific. You really seem to understand the topic."

I felt a warm rush. According to the *Contemporary Teen* article, the highest compliment that an older guy could give a girl was to say that she was smart.

Jason handed me the glue, then turned the pages of the book. "Here it is—'The Human Ear.' "We'll have this fixed in no time."

A tingle ran up my spine as Jason and I worked side by side. He was very precise, which is one of the most important things in science. The more time I spent with him, the more perfect he seemed.

"Mr. Monroe, I have an emergency!" The tingly feeling went away as soon as I heard Glen

Benedict's voice. "I was just home," he said, panting. "My cats ate my science project. I gave two plants the same amount of sunlight and water, but I talked to one of the plants and sang to the other one."

Jason rubbed his chin. "Hmmm. I guess it's too late to start that experiment over." He pulled some science books off a shelf. "Why don't you look through these? They might give you another idea."

"Thanks," Glen said as he sat down at the table right beside me.

By now the ear was fixed. With Glen butting in, there was no use sticking around anymore. As much as I wanted to be with Jason, I couldn't stand the thought of spending any more time with Glen. There was no way Jason would confess his true feelings for me in front of Glen.

I stuck my posters on a shelf, then put Heather's ear back and neatly covered it with the sheet. *Just like new,* I thought with relief.

When I walked back into the classroom, Glen quickly flipped through the pages of the science book while Jason drank coffee. I picked up my backpack.

"I was just thinking about what a great job you did on those posters," Jason told me, looking up. "If I didn't know any better, I'd think that they were done by a professional."

"You mean like someone older than me?" I asked.

"Definitely."

"There's going to be a lot more to my report," I told him excitedly. "I'm going to put together a collage of some of the things that can be made from recycled aluminum, glass, and plastic. Plus, I'm doing this really cool demonstration of how recycling plants separate materials. And—"

"You've really put a lot of thought into this."

"I want to do a good job."

"I can tell. Your family must be pretty proud of you," he said.

I blushed. "I guess so."

"Do you have a big family?" he asked.

I felt my heart skip. For a teacher, that was a pretty *personal* question. When I stayed after school to help Mr. Norris, we always just talked about science—never stuff about my family. Our first talk alone was going just as I'd imagined!

"Well," I said happily, "there's my parents, my grandmother, me, and Yvonne." I scrunched my nose. "And unfortunately, there's also my sister Anne. She had Mr. Norris when she went here."

Behind me Glen sneezed, reminding me why I had been leaving in the first place.

Why don't you leave, Glen, so Jason and I can be alone, I silently willed him.

I must have had some strange power over Glen, because at that moment, he got up from his chair.

"I think I figured out what I'm going to do," Glen said. "I'd better go to the pet store before it closes. See ya later, Mr. Monroe. Bye, Rosie."

"You don't get along very well with Anne?" Jason continued when Glen left the room.

"Not really," I said, trying to sound cheerful even though I was talking about Anne.

"You and Yvonne seem pretty close, though."

"Yeah, Yvonne is totally cool." *Get to the point, Jason,* I begged him silently. *Ask me out.*

Jason cleared his throat as if he was going to say something important. My heart flip-flopped.

"Can I ask you a question?" he finally said.

It was really going to happen! My whole

body felt so light, as though a magic carpet had scooped me up and was taking me higher and higher into the air.

I breathed deeply to hide my excitement. "Sure."

"Does Yvonne have a boyfriend?"

The magic carpet suddenly jerked out from under me, and I crashed to the ground. "You mean my sister?"

Jason's eyes lit up as he nodded eagerly.

I blinked away the tears that were forming in my eyes. I couldn't look like a total baby in front of Jason. And I couldn't stand the thought of his going out with someone else.

"Yes," I lied. "She's engaged." I picked up my backpack and headed toward the door. "Sorry, but I have to go now." Sobs were already forming in my throat, and I just knew I wouldn't be able to hold them back.

Dear Diary,
I feel like I've been punched in the chest. I thought that Jason would automatically love me if he found out what I was like. That's what hurts the most—he knows me better than he

knows Yvonne, and he wants to go out with her. And after I worked so hard to get him to like me!

Hey, I just thought of something. What if Yvonne likes him too? She did go on about how she would have liked him for a teacher. A teacher—ha! Maybe he's the real reason she's coming back for the science fair.

This is so awful. Now I'm not just competing against my best friend in the science fair; I'm competing against my favorite sister in romance!

-R

I shut my diary and put it back in my drawer. Then I got the phone and dialed Yvonne's phone number.

"Hello?" Yvonne answered.

"Hi, it's me," I said cheerfully. I hated being so phony, but if Yvonne suspected that I was upset, she'd want to know why, and I wasn't about to tell her.

"What's up, little sis?"

"I've been thinking. You probably shouldn't come to the science fair. My project is a mess, and I'm kind of embarrassed to show it to you."

"You're just nervous," Yvonne said soothingly. "I'm sure it's going to be the best one there."

"Actually, it probably won't even be finished in time."

"Don't be silly. You still have a whole two weeks left."

Did she have to be so encouraging? "Yeah, well, I'd better go now," I said.

Two weeks, I thought when I'd hung up. *Two whole weeks to convince her not to come.*

Chapter 10

Dear Diary,

I got my braces today, and
Dr. Price said I have to wear
that disgusting headgear. Every
time I put it on, I want to
cry. Even with the six ceramic
brackets, I look totally dweeby.
That's not the only reason I
want to cry. Yvonne still
plans to come to the science
fair.

For the past week I've been
doing practically nothing but
working on my project. Now
that I know Jason likes
Yvonne, it's more important
than ever for me to win the
fair. I have to become his
science buddy so he can see
he chose the wrong Bantan.
It's too bad Yvonne is

coming to the fair. I'll have
to figure out some way to keep
her and Jason apart once
she's here.

One good thing has
happened to me, though. All of
the talk about my braces and
the science fair have made my
parents forget all about the
contribution money. Once I
make it through the science
fair, I can figure out how to
solve that problem.

-R

"Mmmm mmmm!" Anne said at dinner on
Tuesday night. "This is so good, Nanna. You
should try some, Rosie." She stuck a forkful of
eskovitch in front of me. Eskovitch is fried fish
with vinegar, onions, and peppers. The way
Nanna makes it, it's delicious. Tonight I
wouldn't know about that, though. My mouth
was throbbing from my braces, and the fish was
way too spicy for my sore gums. I could hardly
even eat the red pea soup that Nanna had fixed
especially for me.

"Don't you ever shut up?" I snapped at
Anne.

"Geez. You can't even pay someone a compliment without the Metal Queen getting upset."

"I don't think that was a compliment, Anne. That was a comment meant expressly to annoy your sister," Mom said.

My father wiped his mouth with a napkin. "Your mother tells me that you'll be wearing headgear," he said.

"Yeah," I grumbled. "Fourteen hours a day."

"I know you're not happy about it, but I think I've figured out a way to make it work and make you happy," he continued.

I stirred my soup. "How? Wear a paper bag over my head?"

"Nothing that drastic." Dad cleared his throat. "Since you sleep with the headgear about eight hours a night, that leaves just six more hours to wear your headgear during the day. If you'll wear it when you get home from school and when you're home on the weekends, you'll have no problem getting in all ninety-eight hours for the week."

My dad's plan actually sounded pretty good. There had to be some catch, though. "What if I go to the Pop Stop or something after school?"

"*If* you wear it every night and *if* you wear it

at home and at Amy's and Heather's houses after school," my mother began, "we won't make you wear it in public."

"But if you don't wear it when you're at home, you will have to make up the time—even if that means your friends will see you," Dad added.

"All right!" I smiled for the first time all day. All I'd have to do was wear the headgear when my parents were around. They'd never know if I wasn't wearing it at Amy's and Heather's. For once my parents had come up with a rule that was practically torture-free!

As Jason began class the next day, I kept a straight face. There was no way I'd let him see my braces. I was going to hide them from him for as long as possible.

"We're not going to have a lecture today," Jason announced. "Since some of you still have a lot of work to do, I'm going to give you guys a chance to work on your science fair projects."

"Mine's at home," Aaron said, standing up. "I'll go get it."

"I'm sure there is plenty that you can do right here," Jason said firmly, then looked out over the rest of the class. "If you need to get anything out of the storage room, please go ahead." Jason went around the desk and sat down in his chair.

Amy slid her chair away from the table. "Well, I'd better get mine. I have to finish my diorama of a long-jump pit."

I turned around. Heather wasn't moving. "What about you?"

"I finished painting my ears and getting the display ready. Now I just have to train Rexi." Rexi is Heather's Pekingese.

"What's she going to do?"

"Mom bought me a really high-pitched whistle that dogs can hear but people can't. I'm training Rexi to roll over when she hears the noise." If Heather was counting on her dog to win the science fair, I still had a really good chance. Rexi was cute and friendly, but she wasn't exactly cooperative.

"Oh," I said, smiling. "I'm finished too."

By now kids were swarming around Jason's desk, holding up parts of their science fair projects. Everyone was pushing, shoving, and talking at once.

"Please go back to your seats," Jason yelled over the noise. "I'll come around and help you one at a time." The crowd of kids split up and went back to their seats to wait for Jason.

Instead of helping them right away, though, Jason walked over and stopped in the aisle beside Heather and Amy.

I barely looked at him. I didn't want to take any chances. If I opened my mouth too much, all of the metal in the back and on the bottom was really obvious.

"You three seem to be in good shape," Jason began. "You'll really give the other kids some fierce competition."

"Wait until they see my fierce dog," Heather said. "That'll really scare them."

Amy and I started to giggle. Rexi's about as fierce as a fly. She'd probably be afraid of a fly.

When I realized what I was doing, I covered my mouth quickly, but it was too late.

"Hey, did you get braces, Rosie?"

"Mmm hmm." It was the only thing I could say without opening my mouth.

"I almost didn't notice. I like them."

I wrinkled my forehead. "You do?"

"Sure. They're kind of unusual. When I had to wear braces, they had huge silver bands that went all the way around your teeth."

"You had braces?" I asked.

"For three years."

I felt a million times better. Jason actually thought my braces looked nice! And now braces were something else that we had in common.

"I was wondering if you three could help me out," Jason continued. "The science department has some money to spend on decorating the cafeteria for the fair, but I don't have any time—or ideas."

"You want us to be in charge of decorations?" I asked excitedly. The only thing better than my science skill is my decorating skill. I decorated my bedroom all by myself, and it looks really cool. Almost everything is purple, including my beanbag chair. "We could put white sheets on all of the tables," I suggested. "That would make the displays look really nice."

"I saw some old pictures of famous scientists in the storage room," Heather commented. "Maybe Mr. Norris would let us borrow them."

"Excellent!" I smiled. Decorating the cafeteria was a perfect way to show Jason just how multitalented I am.

Chapter 11

"We're going to be late," I said again, tapping my foot nervously. I'd been dressed and ready to go for hours. The night before I had picked out my outfit—a purple T-shirt and a yellow miniskirt, with red dangly earrings. And I was way too nervous to eat breakfast.

My father put down his newspaper. "The science fair doesn't start for another hour," he reminded me.

"That's when the judging starts. I want to get there early to check out the competition." Amy, Heather, and I had stayed after school to help Mr. Norris and Mrs. Patterson decorate the cafeteria, but Ms. Cohen came to get us before the projects were set up.

"Of course Rosie's excited," Yvonne said, walking into the kitchen. "This could be the most important day of her life."

That's right, Yvonne. As long as you don't do anything to ruin it, I told her silently. Then I checked out her outfit—a short black-and-white floral dress with a loose skirt. Her thick black hair was pulled back in a ponytail, showing off her perfect face. She looked great.

"Rosie, why don't you go see if Nanna's ready, and we can leave?" my mother said.

I jumped up. "By the way, where's Anne?"

"She had to go to work early today," Dad explained. "She can't come."

"Cool," I said as I headed out of the kitchen to get my grandmother.

"Don't forget to put your headgear on," Dad added.

I spun around. "You're making me wear my headgear to the science fair? You said I didn't have to wear it in public."

"You remember the rules, Rosie," Dad said. "You haven't worn your headgear for the past two nights."

Drat! I must have forgotten to put it on when I came downstairs to watch TV or something. Either that or my parents had installed hidden cameras in my bedroom. "I'm still getting used to it," I said quickly. "I promise I'll start wearing it as soon as it stops being so uncomfortable."

"Rosie, you know perfectly well that you won't get used to it if you don't wear it," Mom said firmly. "Besides, we made a deal."

"But the deal shouldn't apply to the science fair," I said desperately. "Practically every kid in seventh grade will be there. I can't show up looking like a total geek."

"Rosie, if you had acted more like a seventh grader in the first place and taken some responsibility, this wouldn't have been an issue today," Mom said.

I turned to Yvonne. She was my only hope when it came to my parents' ridiculous rules.

"Oh, come on, Rosie," Yvonne said cheerfully. "You don't look anything remotely like a geek in your headgear. And your teeth will never be fixed if you don't wear it."

"Fine," I mumbled. Completely defeated, I walked down the hall to Nanna's room. *Easy for Yvonne to be cheerful*, I thought. *She's not the one who'll look like a major nerd in front of Jason.*

"Sit, Rexi!" Heather's voice echoed through the Whitman cafeteria.

"Come on, Yvonne, let's go see Heather," I said, grabbing her arm.

The cafeteria was crowded with teachers and families. In a way, that was good, because it would be easier to keep Yvonne and Jason apart. But it also meant that practically everyone in Englewood was seeing me with my headgear on.

By the time we made it over to Heather's display, Ms. Cohen was shaking her finger at Rexi and shouting "Be good!"

Heather looked as though she was about to cry. "Rexi won't behave. She's going to ruin everything."

"No way!" Yvonne said as she looked at Heather's project. "This is really great!"

I had to admit that Yvonne was right. Heather's exhibit was divided into three parts: Why Dogs Hear, What Dogs Hear, and How Dogs Hear. She had drawn a funny cartoon for each section that explained the reasons dogs can hear sounds that human beings can't. It's kind of complex, but Heather made it completely clear.

Heather's round cheeks turned bright red. "I hope I do okay. I got a special whistle that only dogs can hear, and Rexi's supposed to help me show the judges how it works."

When I saw the hopeful look on Heather's face, part of me was glad that she had come up with such a great idea for her project. But the competitive side of me was glad that Rexi was being so horrible. Heather's project was interesting, but without the live demonstration, I had the edge.

Heather leaned closer to me. "I thought you only had to wear your headgear at night."

"My parents are trying to teach me a lesson."

"Oh, well, it's not so bad. The strap looks pretty next to your T-shirt."

That made me feel even worse. Heather was a real friend.

Ms. Cohen came over and scooped up Rexi. The dog tilted her head and gave us an innocent look.

"Mom, this is Rosie's sister Yvonne," Heather told her mom.

"Nice to meet you," Ms. Cohen said, shaking Yvonne's hand. "It's a great fair, isn't it?"

"Actually, it's kind of hard to tell. Rosie won't let me stand anywhere for more than half a second. She keeps rushing me from one display to the next."

"I guess I'm just excited," I said sweetly as I

looked around the cafeteria. Jason was headed right in our direction. "Well, we'd better move on. I'll see you later, Heather."

"Rosie—" Yvonne began as I grabbed her arm.

"There are a lot of projects we haven't seen yet," I broke in as I yanked her so hard she couldn't help but follow me.

Finally, the judges started going from project to project. I stood by mine, keeping my eye on where Yvonne was talking with Nanna and my parents. Jason was safely out of the way, speaking with Mr. Norris and Mrs. Patterson.

My project was in just about the best spot. I was right on the end of a table near the cafeteria doors. Anyone going in or out would be sure to see it.

As I moved around some of the props for my demonstration, I felt a tap on my back. I turned around to see Amy.

"You're wearing a dress!" I said, stunned.

Amy rolled her eyes. "My mom made me. I feel like everyone's staring." She was probably right. Since I had known Amy, she'd worn a dress only three times: when her mom got married again, when her dad got married again, and last year at the sixth grade dress-up dance.

"I know how you feel." I pointed to my headgear. "This isn't really my idea of a great fashion accessory."

"It looks okay."

Just when I was about to tell Amy she should get her eyes checked, Jake Meadows interrupted our conversation.

"Hi, you guys. Amy, I just saw your science project. It's really cool."

"Thanks, Jake," Amy said. "What are you doing here?"

"Shannon wanted me to come look at her project. She's gabbing with some of her friends, so I made my escape." Jake looked at my table and smiled. "Wow! Who helped you with this?"

"No one. I did everything by myself," I explained.

"It's really incredible. You've got a lot of detail, but it's not boring at all."

"Jake!" Shannon called from the next table. "Come look at Wendy's project. It's so adorable."

"I should probably go," Jake said. "I'll catch you guys later."

Amy waved and smiled. "See you later."

"Bye," I said, inspecting my trash collage.

"Did you see his face when he looked at your project?" Amy asked excitedly when Jake had gone. "He was really impressed."

"Mmm hmm," I said as I rearranged some paper clips. "I guess so."

"You *guess* so?" she shrieked. "Jake basically said he *loved* your project. A few weeks ago you would have gone crazy."

I shrugged. "I guess I'm not like that anymore."

"Rosie, I don't know about this Jason thing. I mean, you told us about how he asked about Yvonne...."

"He'll get over it. He thinks she's engaged, remember?"

Amy looked as though she was about to say something else, but instead she just pointed across the room. "Look. It's Heather's turn."

"Let's get closer," I suggested as three judges surrounded Heather and Rexi.

"What pitch can human beings normally hear?" the first judge asked.

"Uh...adults"—Heather swallowed hard—"hear...um...from sixteen to twenty thousand cycles per...um...second."

"And dogs?" another judge asked as she wrote something down on her clipboard.

"Well, they...uh...forty thousand cycles per second."

"She's really nervous," Amy whispered anxiously.

"Maybe Rexi will do all right," I suggested. As hard as I tried, it was tough to think of Heather as just another competitor when she was so scared.

Finally, the judges stopped asking questions. It was time for Heather to demonstrate the results of her study.

"Rexi, sit," Heather commanded. Miraculously, Rexi obeyed, and Heather rewarded her with a biscuit.

Heather and I took a deep breath at the same time as she lifted her whistle to her lips.

"Hey, Freddy, come back here!" Glen Benedict's high voice echoed over the whole cafeteria. I turned to see Glen diving under a table. "There he is!" Glen shouted as the frog he was using for his new science fair project bobbed away from his display. I had to laugh at the face of horror on Shannon, who was standing near Glen's table.

"Augh!" she screamed, as Freddy jumped past her. "Get that thing away from me!"

Aaron and his friends Peter Martin and Josh

Lefkowitz raced over to help Glen capture Freddy. Suddenly Rexi leaped off the table and ran after the escaped frog, too!

"Rexi! Stop!" Heather yelled. Rexi didn't listen.

"Oh, no! Grab her before she eats Freddy!" Glen screamed.

Soon Freddy, Rexi, Glen, Heather, Mr. Norris, Ms. Cohen, a group of seventh graders, and some parents were racing down the cafeteria.

"Where did the frog go?" Ms. Cohen asked, looking defeated.

"I don't know," Glen said breathlessly, spinning around in circles.

"Maybe you should follow Rexi," Heather suggested weakly. But Rexi looked as if she had given up on Freddy. She was sitting by Mrs. Patterson's feet, barking.

Suddenly, Mrs. Patterson screamed. Freddy jumped out from her nest of hair, which she wore teased on top of her head, right onto the chair next to Shannon! Shannon screamed even louder than Mrs. Patterson had and ran out of the cafeteria. It was like something out of a horror movie.

"Bad frog!" Glen scolded, grabbing Freddy.

Heather scooped up Rexi and hurried over

to her display. But the judges had already moved on to the next project.

"Poor Heather," Amy said, sighing. "She must be so embarrassed."

"Yeah," I agreed, still a little dazed from everything that had just happened. I wished I could have been psyched about seeing Shannon freak out or relieved that my biggest competition had suffered a setback. But I felt too sorry for Heather to be glad.

"Thanks for staying with me," I said to Yvonne as we waited for the judges. "I feel much better with you standing here right next to me."

"You don't have to keep thanking me. It's natural for you to be nervous. I'm just glad I can be here for you."

The judges had only two projects left to look at before it was my turn. My palms sweated as I thought about my presentation, but at least I could relax about Yvonne. Since my parents were off somewhere talking to other parents, I had convinced her that I couldn't survive without her. She wouldn't be off searching for Jason.

But that doesn't mean he won't find her! I panicked as he headed straight for us. *Or me—in my headgear.*

"I'm fine now," I told Yvonne. "You don't have to hang around anymore."

Yvonne looked puzzled. "What are you talking about? I *want* to stay."

"No, really, Yvonne," I insisted. "I've been dragging you around all day. You should go check out Larry Wong's airplane project. See it over there across the room?"

"Poor Rosie. You're so nervous. Listen, your project is the only one I came to see."

Jason was getting closer. If I couldn't make Yvonne leave, at least I could get rid of my headgear. I reached up to unhook the neck strap. That's when I saw Nanna's smiling face coming from the other direction—with Mom and Dad right behind her!

Why me? I wondered as Jason, Nanna, and my parents all rushed over at once.

My head felt as though it was going to burst as I watched two weeks of scheming go down the tubes. Jason would find out that Yvonne wasn't engaged and refuse to accept my lying, headgeared self as his science buddy.

Well, Yvonne and my parents may humiliate me, but I'm not going to embarrass myself! Quickly, I pulled the headgear out of my mouth.

Everyone else greeted one another and shook hands. Then Jason smiled at me. "Rosie, I really want to thank you for all of your help putting this fair together. I've been trying to tell you all morning, but every time I spotted you, you disappeared."

My parents laughed. "That's our Rosie," Dad said. "Always full of energy."

"You must be very proud of her," Jason said. "She's going to be a wonderful scientist someday. I wish everyone cared as much about the environment." He put his strong arm around my shoulder.

"Thanks," I said, glowing all over. "I really enjoyed doing it." This was turning out to be the most perfect day of my life. My parents hadn't asked about my missing headgear, and Jason had barely even *looked* at my sister.

And unless my luck ran out, I'd probably win the science fair—and Jason and I would finally be together forever!

Chapter 12

As the three judges circled my recycling display, I blocked out everything else in the cafeteria. Jason had gone off to show a boy I didn't recognize around the fair, and my family was talking to Amy's and Heather's parents so that they wouldn't make me nervous by hanging around. But I was unbelievably nervous anyway as the judges made notes on their clipboards. So far, they had told me only their names.

After what seemed like an hour, they turned to one another and nodded. "Is there anything you'd like to demonstrate before we ask our questions?" Mrs. Koblenz asked.

I stood up perfectly straight. "Yes. I'd like to show you how a recycling plant uses the physical properties of different materials to separate recyclables."

I took a shoebox that I'd filled with trash and emptied it on the table. There were pieces of aluminum foil, a rubber band, part of a straw, and a few paper clips.

Next, I rubbed a balloon against my top until it felt as though it had a fuzzy invisible coating. I held the balloon about six inches from the pile. A small rubber band jumped onto the side of the balloon.

"The rubber was attracted to the static electricity on the outside of the balloon," I explained.

I picked up a magnet and passed it over the remaining items. The paper clips immediately clung to the magnet. "Magnets attract steel."

Finally, I placed the aluminum and straw in a small bowl of water. The straw floated to the top, but the aluminum sank to the bottom.

"All of these things are recyclable," I explained. "However, not all plants recycle everything, so they have to come up with systems to separate out what they want. They build big equipment that does what I just did."

"Very impressive," said the judge named Mr. Cabrera. "You've done a very nice job explaining *how* to recycle different materials. Would you please tell us *why* people should recycle?"

"There are a thousand good reasons," I said. "But the reason I think is most important is that garbage pollutes the earth—the air, the water, and the ground. A glass bottle takes three thousand years to decompose. We'd eliminate a lot of waste if we recycled glass bottles instead of throwing them out."

"You've obviously researched this thoroughly," the last judge, Mr. Day, said.

"It's been a real pleasure, Rosie," Mrs. Koblenz said finally. "No matter what happens today, I hope you'll keep pursuing your interest in the environment."

No matter what happens today? My head spun faster than ever as the judges walked away. Thanks to Rexi's bad behavior and the fact that I did everything right, didn't I deserve to win?

Heather and Amy rushed over. "Boy, I thought they'd never stop asking questions," Amy said, tugging on the collar of her dress.

"Were you nervous?" Heather asked me.

"I was. Then I wasn't. Now I am."

"I was and I still am. Augh!" Heather shuddered.

Amy and I laughed, and I felt a little less jittery.

"Oh, look," Amy said, pointing. "Jason's going to say something."

He was standing on the small stage at the end of the lunchroom. "I'm very pleased you all made it today. I'd especially like to thank the judges and all of the students for making this a very exciting science fair."

Applause, whistles, and hoots filled the room.

"Now I have to ask you all to leave so that the judges can post the ribbons," Jason continued when the noise died down. "Anyone who is interested in seeing the results may return in an hour."

My family, Ms. Cohen, and Amy's mom and stepfather, Paul Spinosa, crossed the cafeteria toward us. Seeing Yvonne no longer made me nervous. Soon she'd be out of Jason's sight—and things could get back to normal between us. And, hopefully, better than normal between me and Jason.

Our families beamed, and Mom gave me and my two best friends a hug. "You girls were wonderful," she said. "I bet it will be a three-way tie."

Unfortunately, I knew there wasn't even going to be a two-way tie. Only one person could win the grand prize. All of the pressure made the butterflies in my stomach come back.

There was only one place in the world where I'd be able to calm down. "Do you guys want to go to the Pop Stop?" I asked my friends.

"Sure," Amy and Heather responded at the same time.

"I'll come home after the results are posted," Heather told her mother.

"Me too," Amy added to her mom and Paul.

Dad pulled some money out of his wallet. "The Pop Stop is my treat." He leaned closer and in a low voice said, "We'll talk about your headgear later, young lady."

"Thanks, Dad," I said, taking the money and giving him a kiss on the cheek. "Do you want to come with us, Yvonne?"

"I think I'll head home too. But promise you'll let us know right away."

"I will," I said, then hurried out of the cafeteria with my friends.

"Your dad wasn't mad that you took off your headgear?" Kristen asked as she absentmindedly braided a section of her hair. She and Lucy had invited us to sit with them at the Pop Stop.

"I wouldn't say that. I'll probably get in trouble when I get home," I admitted. "But now I've got other things to worry about."

Lucy scrunched her nose. "Too bad about what happened with Glen's frog," she told Heather.

Heather took a sip of her Blueberry Bonanza and smiled. "That's okay. Rexi did look pretty hysterical running after Freddy like that."

"No one looked more ridiculous than Shannon," Amy said. We all laughed.

"So you're not upset about what happened?" I asked Heather.

"Seeing *certain* people make total fools of themselves made the disaster easier to take."

Amy held up her Orange Smoothie. "I'm just glad it's all over!"

The rest of us cheered as we clinked our glasses against hers in a toast.

As I took a sip of my Mango Miracle, Monica Sandborn appeared in the double doors of the Pop Stop. My good mood suddenly vanished. Seeing her only reminded me that I still hadn't figured out a way to come up with the rain forest money.

"You're just the person I wanted to see," Monica said as she approached our table. "I'm going to mail in the money for our acre of rain forest. Do you have your donation with you?"

"Sorry. I didn't bring it."

"Oh. Well, maybe my dad could bring me by your house sometime this weekend, so the money will go out first thing Monday morning."

"Um, this weekend really isn't good. My sister's visiting, so we're doing family stuff the whole weekend."

Monica gave a little sigh. "You can just bring it to school on Monday then. See you guys later." She walked away and sat down at a table with two other eighth-grade girls.

"So what now?" Amy asked me.

"I'll figure out what to do on Monday."

"She's going to keep bugging you about it unless you give her the money," Heather pointed out.

"You're right. I guess I might as well tell her now." I slowly went over to Monica's table.

"Can I talk to you about something?" I asked her.

She looked up. "Sure."

"Um, I'd rather tell you in private."

Monica looked around the Pop Stop. "There really isn't too much privacy here. You can talk in front of these guys."

"Well, okay." I took a deep breath. "I don't

have the fifty dollars anymore. I spent it. I only have about seven bucks left."

Monica frowned.

"So are you going to borrow the money from your parents or something?"

"Actually, that wouldn't be a very good idea."

"I don't get it. What exactly are you saying?" Monica asked.

"That I can't contribute any extra money to the rain forest."

Monica stared at me. "Are you kidding? Now we don't have enough money to buy an acre of rain forest."

"We can still make a donation," I suggested.

"Unless we buy an entire acre, we won't own a piece of the rain forest. A contribution's just not the same."

How could I disagree with Monica when I had said practically the same thing to Amy and Heather just a couple weeks before? I had been the one to get the club psyched about the project. Now I was the one who was going to ruin it for them.

"I'll get the money," I promised. "Somehow."

"I really hope so," Monica said. "The environment club is counting on you."

I trudged over to my table. My friends were

all getting up. "It's been an hour," Heather told me. "Let's go back to the fair now."

My heart raced as I held the cafeteria door open for my friends. They rushed past me. In a few seconds, I would know if I had won and if Jason and I would be together.

I almost fainted when I stepped through the doors and saw the ribbon on my display. I blinked twice to make sure I wasn't imagining it, then hurried through the tables to my best friends. Both of them were waiting by Heather's project.

"I got an honorable mention!" Amy shouted, holding up her white ribbon.

"Great!" I said, hugging her. "How'd you do, Heather?"

She pointed to the shiny red ribbon stuck to her model human ear. "Second place," she said.

"Yay!" I said, relieved that Rexi hadn't completely ruined it for her.

"Well?" Amy said, raising her eyebrows at me.

"I won!" I yelled, throwing my arms around my best friends. The three of us jumped around in a circle.

I had a double reason to celebrate—I was

officially the best seventh-grade science student, *and* I was going to be science buddies with Jason Monroe!

"Where is everyone?" I shouted from the foyer of my house.

"We're down here," Mom called. I raced down the stairs to the family room. My parents, Nanna, and Yvonne were sitting around a game board. Everyone stared at me.

"Guess what? I won!" I waved the blue ribbon in front of my family's faces.

"That's my girl. I'm so proud of you," Mom said, jumping up to hug me.

"You really worked hard, and it paid off," Dad added.

Nanna wrapped her arms around me. "Of course you won. That's because you had the best project."

Yvonne stood up and put her hands on her hips. "Now *you* can congratulate *me*."

"What for?" I asked her.

"On my *engagement*, of course."

"Your engagement?" I asked in a high voice. I felt my face get hot. *Please don't let this mean what I think it means.*

"Funny that you seem so surprised—since

you knew about it before I did. You and Jason, that is."

"Jason thinks you're engaged? Really?" My voice was getting smaller and smaller.

Yvonne groaned. "Give it up, Rosie. We ran into Jason in the parking lot."

I cleared my throat. "And, uh, I guess you told him you weren't getting married."

"Bingo!" Yvonne said.

"You put your sister in a very awkward situation," Mom said.

Dad frowned. "I think you owe Yvonne an explanation."

I slumped down on the couch and crossed my arms. *Oh, great! Not only does Jason know I lied, but now my parents expect me to tell them why.*

I could hardly look at Yvonne. "You're not...going to go on a...date with him, are you?"

"Well, we did make some casual plans for dinner tonight," Yvonne said, sitting down next to me. "But you're invited too."

Was she kidding?

My eyes burned as I tried to hold back tears. "You don't have to feel sorry for me.'

"We're inviting you because we think it

would be more fun with you there," she added.

"I'm sure you and Jason wouldn't want me to butt in on your big date," I said bitterly.

"It's not a 'big' date, Rosie. Jason's bringing someone too, and you wouldn't be butting in. We want you there."

All kinds of thoughts bounced around in my head. I hated Jason for liking Yvonne. I hated Yvonne for being so perfect and wonderful. And I loved them both so much that it hurt to hate them.

Yvonne gently touched my hand, and I felt my eyes fill with tears. *After everything I did, she still cares about me. She even wants me along on her date.*

Why did Yvonne have to be so nice when I wanted to be mad at her? I jumped off the couch and ran upstairs to my room.

Dear Diary,
    Nothing makes sense anymore. Why does loving someone have to feel so good one minute and so crummy the next? And why do I still love Jason so much even though he doesn't like me?
    I can't bear to let Jason

go just like that. Maybe I
should go to dinner with
them. Yvonne did say it
wasn't a big date. Maybe I
still have a chance.

                              -R

Chapter 13

"Mom, have you seen my blue shoes?" Yvonne called, racing down the hall. "We're supposed to be at the restaurant in ten minutes."

"I'm still looking for your earring," Mom called to her. "You've only been here a day. How could you lose so much?"

"I don't get it," she said in frustration. "I was sure I had everything in my room."

"It's not under here," I shouted, hiding my smile as I peered under the couch. *Sorry, Yvonne, but it's for your own good. You'll have to wear sneakers tonight, because I hid one of your good shoes where you'll never find it—unless you dig through my dirty clothes hamper.*

I felt a little bad, but I couldn't help doing it. If I still had a chance with Jason, I needed to look good. And I couldn't look good if Yvonne looked great.

Anne walked down the hall holding a pair of beige shoes with low heels—her best ones. "I didn't find your stuff, but these go with your dress." She handed Yvonne the shoes and a pair of tiny silver earrings. "And these earrings will look really great."

"I owe you big time," Yvonne said, smiling.

Darn it! I huffed silently. *Anne sabotages me even when she isn't trying.* I got up off my knees and went back to my bedroom to check myself out in my full-length mirror. Even *with* the right clothes, Yvonne would have a tough time competing with me tonight. I was wearing a multi-colored striped skirt, a loose white blouse, red tights, and a pair of leather boots that laced just above my ankles.

Two minutes later Yvonne stood in my doorway. A big silver barrette held her thick black ponytail. Anne's shoes looked perfect with Yvonne's flowing rose dress. And she had applied her makeup in record time. As usual, my older sister looked fabulous.

"I'm sorry you had to wait," Yvonne apologized. "Let's go."

"We're meeting two other people here," Yvonne told the host at Pedro's.

The woman picked up four menus. "Right this way," she said.

"Who are we meeting besides Jason?" I asked my sister as we walked through the restaurant.

"You'll see," Yvonne said.

As we approached our table, I got my answer. Next to Jason was a guy who looked about my age. He had curly brown hair and dark eyes, and his face was familiar. But I was almost positive he didn't go to Whitman.

"Enjoy your meal," the host said, placing a menu on each of our plates.

"Hi, Yvonne, Rosie. You look really nice," Jason said. He pulled Yvonne's chair out for her, hardly taking his eyes off of her to smile at me. This wasn't a promising start. I'd have to act fast if I was going to keep Jason from falling too far under my sister's spell.

"Rosie, this is my cousin Derek," Jason introduced us.

"Hi," I said. Then I noticed Yvonne and Jason exchange a little look.

I get it, I thought, my heart sinking. *I've already lost! This guy is supposed to be my consolation prize. Yvonne got the grand prize, and I'm supposed to be satisfied with his cousin.*

Yvonne opened her menu, then turned to

Jason. "I'm so sorry we're late. It was all my fault. Rosie had to wait forever for me."

"That's all right," Jason assured her. "The only thing that matters is that you made it." His dark brown eyes sparkled at Yvonne.

Nice, Jason, I thought. *You don't have to be so obviously ga-ga over her.*

Derek picked up his menu. "I'm starved."

"The worst part about eating at Pedro's is deciding what to order," Jason said.

Yvonne scanned her menu. "It all sounds delicious. I love Mexican food."

"Me too." Jason smiled at her. Yvonne half-giggled.

Puke. Did I have to sit here all night watching the two of them swoon at each other? I sat stiffly in my chair. I was getting madder and madder.

Derek peered at me over the top of his menu. "Aren't you going to eat anything?" he asked.

"I already know what I'm going to get." What could be messier than a sloppy bean burrito smothered in cheese? Maybe some of it would land on Yvonne's lap.

"Me too," Jason commented, closing his menu. "It's the same thing I always get—tacos."

"You get tacos every time?" I asked.

"They're so good I can't resist."

Very adventurous! I thought sarcastically.

The waiter approached our table. "Are you ready to order?" he asked.

When we were done ordering our food and drinks, I turned to Jason.

"So, has Yvonne told you about the time she stuck a dime up her nose and had to be rushed to the emergency room?"

"Rosie! I don't think we need to talk about that right now," Yvonne said sternly.

"Rosie, Derek's in seventh grade too," Jason said urgently.

"I go to Old Dominion Academy," Derek explained. Old Dominion Academy is a private school in Englewood.

"Oh," I said, without looking at Derek. I racked my brain for more embarrassing things to tell Jason about Yvonne.

Then the waiter came with our drinks. He stood between my sister and me and started to place them on the table. Suddenly, I had an inspiration. Why should I wait till our food got here? The sooner I stopped the evening from getting goopier than I could stand, the better.

"Excuse me. Where's the bathroom?" I

asked, bumping the waiter as I stood up.

"Augh!" Yvonne screamed as the cold drinks hit her lap. She jumped up, grabbed her napkin, and wiped herself off.

Busboys rushed over. Yvonne hurried away to the ladies' room.

I buried my face in my hands. "I feel awful," I said, trying to sound convincing.

"It was an accident," Jason said. "It could have happened to anyone."

"I hope Yvonne isn't mad at me."

"I don't think Yvonne's like that," Jason said, dipping his half-eaten chip into the salsa bowl.

Oh, please, you act as if you know her better than I do. I had to admit, though, that he was probably right. Yvonne *wasn't* really mad at me. I started to regret what I'd done.

"I was in the Science Buddy program last year," Derek said. "It's really great."

"Yeah, I'm sure," I said dully. If anyone thought I was going to get excited by anything that Mr. Consolation Prize had to say, they were nuts.

"Could you pass the salsa, please?" I asked.

Jason picked up the bowl and held it in front of me. I reached out to take it as he turned to face the bathroom doors. The next thing I knew, he let go of the salsa, which slipped through my hands and landed all over me!

"This is my best skirt!" I cried.

"I'm so sorry," Jason said, looking stunned. "I thought you had a grip on it."

Maybe if you hadn't been looking for Yvonne with your moon eyes, you'd have thought otherwise. I stormed off to the bathroom.

When I entered through the swinging doors Yvonne was holding the skirt of her dress under the hand dryer. "What happened to you?" she asked.

"Klutzy Jason dropped the bowl of salsa on me." I wiped the mess with some paper towels.

"Too bad my dress is almost dry. I could have squeezed it onto your skirt. Seltzer water's supposed to get almost anything out." She looked as though she was trying to hold back laughter.

"I don't think it's very funny that Jason ruined my favorite outfit," I told her.

"I'm sure it was just an accident, Rosie. Just like you *accidentally* spilled the drinks on me. Right?" She raised her eyebrows at me. "I know you pretty well, Rosie, and I'm guessing that the missing shoe wasn't exactly an accident either, huh?"

Suddenly I was really tired—tired of lying,

tired of chasing after Jason, and most of all tired of messing up things for Yvonne. I looked at my hands. "I guess all that spilling business was pretty obvious."

"About as obvious as the fact that I wanted to see Jason at the science fair."

"I knew it!" I said.

Yvonne held her hands up in front of herself. "That was only a teeny part of the reason I came, though. I really miss you when I'm at school. And since I'm so dense, I thought you wanted me at the science fair. I had no idea there were *two* competitions going on."

Yvonne really *did* know me well—a lot better than I knew Jason, that was for sure. In fact, the more I got to know Jason, the more my plan to come between him and Yvonne just didn't seem worth it.

"I'm really glad you came," I told her. "And I'm sorry I tried to mess everything up for you. At least we're even now." I held out my stained skirt.

"Does that mean you're not mad about Jason and me?"

"I guess not," I said softly. "I mean, I still think he's cute and everything, but maybe he's more your type than mine. He took a bite off his chip and dipped it back in the salsa. Yuck!"

Yvonne laughed. "Well, I'm not quite so picky." She wet a paper towel and helped me clean up.

We walked back to the table, and Jason's face lit up when he saw Yvonne. "Beautiful as ever," he said.

Corny as ever, I thought.

"Rosie, I'll give you the money for the dry cleaning," Jason told me.

"That's all right. It was just an accident," I said, shooting Yvonne a knowing look. "It could have happened to anyone."

"So, anything exciting happen while we were gone?" Yvonne asked.

"We were talking about Rosie's science project, actually," Jason said.

"It was really cool," Derek commented. "I knew it would win as soon as I saw it."

"Really?" I asked, turning toward him for the first time all night. He was actually pretty cute—not gorgeous like Jake Meadows, but cute. "Hey, I know where I've seen you! You're the guy Jason—Mr. Monroe—was showing around this morning."

Derek nodded. "I especially liked the diagram on your poster that showed how garbage hurts waterlife. I want to be a marine biologist."

"You want to be a scientist too?"

"Yeah, that's why Jason invited me to the fair. I'm afraid that by the time I go to college, though, all of the fish might be dead."

"If people just started thinking about their trash before they threw it out, the earth would be a lot cleaner."

"Listen, I just thought of something," Derek said. "I'm in a club that's going on a trip to clean up the James River. It's mostly adults. It would more fun with someone else my age. Do you want to go?"

I could feel Jason and Yvonne smiling at me intently, but I didn't really care. "Sure," I told Derek. "It sounds like fun."

"Derek's really cool. I'm glad I met him," I told Yvonne the next morning.

She threw her overnight bag into the trunk of her car and gave me a mischievous smile. "He's pretty cute, too, don't you think?"

"Well, sure," I said. "But I don't really feel that way about him. We might get to be good friends, that's all."

"I'm glad you guys hit it off. When I met him at the science fair, I knew you'd get along."

"There's something else I wanted to tell you."

"Yeah?"

"You and Mr. Monroe make a good couple."

"Thanks, Rosie. He's a really nice guy." From the glow on her face, I could tell she thought he was more than just a nice guy.

"He's really into you—and he's a great teacher. I'm sorry I tried to mess things up between you two."

"That's okay," she said. "I think it worked out for all of us."

I gave Yvonne a big hug, careful not to bump her with my headgear. (After we got back from the restaurant, I decided it was easier to follow my parents' rules than suffer two years of looking like a geek in public.)

Suddenly, Nanna threw open the front door. "Don't forget these," she shouted to Yvonne. "I baked you a batch of chocolate chip cookies."

Yvonne took the box and kissed Nanna on the cheek. "What are you trying to do, make me fat?"

"You could use some meat on these bones." Our grandmother pinched Yvonne's slim waist.

Yvonne gave Mom and Dad a kiss, then climbed into her car.

We all waved and shouted good-bye as she pulled out of the driveway and drove down the street.

"Are there any cookies left?" Anne asked Nanna as soon as Yvonne's car was out of sight.

"Of course. You don't think I'd forget about you two, do you?"

Anne and I started to race for the front door. But I stopped cold when I felt my father's firm hand on my shoulder.

"Just a minute, young lady," he said.

Uh oh. That doesn't sound good.

Hesitantly, I turned to face him and my mom. That's when I noticed the bag in my mother's hand.

"Um, what's that?" I asked carefully.

"It's makeup," Mom said. "I was checking under your bed for dirty clothes, and I found it."

"I'm sorry. I only wore it a few days, and I'm never going to wear it again—until I'm older."

"That's not what I'm worried about right now," my mother said. "This is a very expensive brand. How could you afford all of these things?"

"Well…um…" It was no use. I had to come clean. I'd done enough lying and covering up for a while. "I used the money that Grandmom and

Grandpop gave me." I hung my head. "I meant to donate half of it to the environment club so that we could buy some rain forest, but everything got all messed up." I took a deep breath and waited for my punishment.

"Okay, Rosie," Mom finally said. "We'll loan you the money to donate to the environment club."

"You will?"

"*But*," Dad said firmly, "you'll have to spend at least one day every weekend collecting recycling until you've earned it back."

"That's impossible. I'll be fifty years old before I can collect that many cans and bottles. And what about—"

"The other half will come out of your allowance," Mom added sternly.

"But—"

"We think we're being very reasonable with you, Rosie," Mom interrupted. "Especially considering *all* the ways you've been sneaking around lately." She peered at my headgear to show what she meant.

Then my parents started walking toward the house. As usual, they'd made up their minds. I could forget about negotiating.

"You look bummed. What's up?" Heather

asked as she and Amy came over from Amy's house.

"Oh, nothing," I said, sighing. "I'll get over it."

"We're going to the game room at the Community Center," Amy said. "Want to come?"

"Let's go to the Pop Stop instead. I heard Jake's going to be there."

Heather's eyes bugged open. "You want to see Jake Meadows?"

"Why not? He *is* the cutest guy at Whitman."

I unhooked my headgear and skipped down the street with my very best friends.

Dear Diary,
    Even though it was tons of hard work, winning the science fair was really fun. I learned a lot about trash, but I learned a lot more about love. You can't really make someone love you by wearing makeup or winning the science fair. Love just happens.
    I can't believe how wrong I was about Jason's older-guy signals and body language. I'm going to write a complaint to <u>Contemporary Teen</u>.

It's still my favorite
magazine, but sometimes those
writers don't know what
they're talking about.

I'm glad that things are
back to normal with Yvonne
and me. She's still the best
sister ever. Working side by
side with Jason won't exactly
be the most romantic
experience, but I bet he'll
make a great science buddy.

-R

Don't miss Diary S.O.S. #4 :

IS IT A CRIME TO BE COOL?

Dear Diary:
I can't believe what happened in school today! I almost got caught for helping two girls in my social studies class, Lara and Deirdre, cheat on the exam. But Mrs. Sud believed me when I lied and told her we'd all studied together. And she never even suspected me when the three of us put that spider in her drawer!

Now I'm figuring out that the whole world won't come crashing down if I do something bad. It was even kind of exciting to get away with that stuff today, even if it was wrong.

Besides, I like Lara and Deirdre. People think they're tough, but when I'm with them, I don't feel like shy little Heather. For once, I feel like a somebody.

—Heather

You've met Amy, Heather, and Rosie...
Now meet the girls at the

Jina, Andie, Lauren, and Mary Beth—the four roommates in Suite 4B at Foxhall Academy, may not see eye to eye on everything. But they do agree on one thing: they love horses! You'll want to read all the books in this extra-special new series.

#1 • A Horse for Mary Beth
Mary Beth can't wait to get to boarding school. But she never expected that all her classmates would be such serious riders. Trying to fit in, Mary Beth signs up for the junior riding program, but she's absolutely petrified. How will she ever keep her new friends from finding out she's scared of horses?

#2 • Andie Out of Control
Andie Perez loves a challenge—and right now it's to get kicked out of yet another boarding

school. She horrifies her roommates by breaking practically every rule in the Foxhall Student Handbook. Then a wild young Thoroughbred named Magic arrives at the school stables, and Andie decides she wants to stay. But it may be too late—for both Andie and Magic!

#3 • Jina Rides to Win

Jina Williams is one of the best riders at Foxhall Academy. She even boards her own horse at the school stables. Jina knows that she and Superstar can win the Junior Working Hunter Horse of the Year Award. But when she pushes herself and her horse too hard, disaster strikes. Now Jina never wants to ride again...

and coming soon:

#4 • Lessons for Lauren